"Stop! Federal agen[t]"

Linc shoved the door open and jumped o̶u̶t the truck, holding his pistol low as he stepped forward.

The dark figure froze.

With a scream that echoed off the trees, Angie drove her foot back and swept the man's leg from under him.

They tumbled to the ground in a heap.

Angie rolled to the side, scrambled to her feet and stood over the figure as though she was going to fight for her life.

"Angie! Back away!" The closer she was to her assailant, the more she risked injury.

Angie eased toward the porch.

When he was about fifteen feet away, Linc stopped and raised his SIG toward the man's center mass as he lay on his back. "Federal agent. Get on your stomach and lace your fingers behind your head."

For a second, the scene froze as though someone had hit the pause button. The only sound was Linc's breathing, short and quick. The next few seconds could change all of their lives. Everything hinged on what the shadowy stranger did next.

Jodie Bailey writes novels about freedom and the heroes who fight for it. Her novel *Crossfire* won a 2015 RT Reviewers' Choice Best Book Award. She is convinced a camping trip to the beach with her family, a good cup of coffee and a great book can cure all ills. Jodie lives in North Carolina with her husband, her daughter and two dogs.

Books by Jodie Bailey

Love Inspired Suspense

Dead Run
Calculated Vendetta
Fatal Response
Mistaken Twin
Hidden Twin
Canyon Standoff
"Missing in the Wilderness"
Fatal Identity
Under Surveillance
Captured at Christmas
Witness in Peril
Blown Cover
Deadly Vengeance
Undercover Colorado Conspiracy
Hidden in the Canyon

Rocky Mountain K-9 Unit

Defending from Danger

Pacific Northwest K-9 Unit

Olympic Mountain Pursuit

Visit the Author Profile page at LoveInspired.com for more titles.

Hidden in the Canyon

JODIE BAILEY

LOVE INSPIRED SUSPENSE
INSPIRATIONAL ROMANCE

LOVE INSPIRED® SUSPENSE

INSPIRATIONAL ROMANCE

ISBN-13: 978-1-335-59807-3

Hidden in the Canyon

Recycling programs
for this product may
not exist in your area.

Love Inspired
22 Adelaide St. West, 41st Floor
Toronto, Ontario M5H 4E3, Canada
www.LoveInspired.com

Printed in Lithuania

MIX
Paper | Supporting
responsible forestry
FSC® C021394

He shall not be afraid of evil tidings:
his heart is fixed, trusting in the Lord.
—*Psalms* 112:7

To Emily

Thank you for believing in this Army wife's stories

ONE

At least the protestors seemed to have taken the night off.

Angie Garcia slowed to a stop at the gate to her family's ranch near the south rim of the Grand Canyon and allowed herself one small sigh of relief. At nearly three in the morning, after a four-hour drive and a night that had gone entirely sideways, she was in no mood to engage with a group of people who wanted her gone.

The signs of their presence remained, though.

Literal signs, propped along the fence.

The Canyon Belongs to Everyone!

No More Tourists!

And her personal favorite: *Stop Destroying the Land!*

That was the exact opposite of what she was working to do on Fairweather Ranch. As a meteorologist, she'd studied how weather and the environment worked together, how man could protect or ravage the environment they held dear. The *environment* included the land itself. Her goal was to preserve, not to destroy. To educate, not to harm. The protestors would understand if they'd talk to her instead of making assumptions and spreading rumors.

For three weeks they'd dogged her gate, making her the unexpected target of their misdirected outrage.

She punched the remote in her car to open the electric gate and drove through, making sure it closed behind her. There had been two instances of vandalism on the property in the previous week, perpetrated by a couple of the protestors. The last thing she needed was a repeat.

Navigating the road through stands of trees on the edge of the Kaibab National Forest, it was too easy to imagine eyes were on her. People lurking in the darkness… Protestors in the shadows waiting…watching.

This shouldn't be how she had to live, looking over her shoulder, wondering if someone was going to do more damage to the ranch she loved. Her family had been gracious and kind to the people who wanted them to return their pocket of privately owned land to the federal government for conservation. The escalation to trespassing and vandalism in the previous weeks had been jarring.

Angie shuddered and gripped the wheel tighter. Paranoia was not her friend, and it was likely the result of high-running emotions and lack of sleep. What she needed was her bed and sleep to forget her name hadn't been called tonight in Vegas for the half-million-dollar Celeste Hyacinthe scientific research grant.

No, it hadn't been her name broadcast through the microphone to nearly a thousand of her peers. Instead, she'd been slapped by the name of the one person she'd never wanted to lose to. Had been forced to clap for his success…and her very public failure.

Surely the reason she felt like she was being watched in the dark isolation near her home was because she was certain every eye had been on her as Owen Matthews took the stage to accept the money on behalf of his environmental research foundation, Crucial Causes.

She forced herself to breathe and to focus on reality. There were no prying eyes on her property, and she was safe. One of the protestors, Monica Huerta, had been a high-school classmate. Though they'd lost touch over the past decade and a half, Monica had promised Angie at church the previous Sunday that the group had rooted out the vandals and would keep things from escalating further.

At the moment, she was too emotionally wrung out to put coherent thoughts into place. She needed sleep. Quiet. A few minutes to ask God what in the world He was thinking. He knew what she needed to run the research center that was her dream. Why hadn't He provided?

She slowed to make the turn into the drive to the house, but her foot shifted to the brake.

The hairs on the back of her neck stood up.

The night felt different. Strange.

In the distance, about a mile away, the glow from the scattered buildings at the ranch's research center softened the edges of the darkness. Ellis West was the only one there tonight, taking care of the horses in the large ranch barn and preparing to ride out to move their small herd of cattle. Her manager, Rosa Boyd, had gone to visit her mother, who was recovering from a stroke, while two of the other ranch hands were also visiting family. The researchers who were staying on the property were all on an excursion into the canyon.

To her right, the exterior lights on her brother's cabin shone from half a mile away, even though he wasn't home.

Nothing was wrong, yet something felt different.

She let the SUV coast toward her home. The light above the garage offered a welcoming circle of warmth. The floodlights on the small horse barn behind the house lit the paddock. The barn was empty at the moment. Her horse, Flynn, and her brother's horse, Shiloh, were being temporarily stabled at the large barn at the main ranch with the working horses to make it easier for the hands to care for them during her absence.

Rolling to a stop close to the house, she scanned the area, still feeling as though someone was watching her.

Automatically, her hand moved to her phone to call her brother, but Jacob was on the other side of the Atlantic with his wife and young daughter, celebrating their two-year anniversary as a family.

She tapped the phone, staring at the pattern of her headlights on the white garage door as tinges of unease prickled along her spine. She still had Lincoln Tucker's number saved, though she'd hovered over the delete button more than once. Because he was Jacob's closest friend and his team leader with the National Park Service Investigative Services Branch, she'd kept it in case of emergency.

Well, a shudder down her spine was definitely not grounds for making a call into the past. She pulled her hand from the phone. She'd been drained by her past enough for one night.

There was nothing odd going on, other than exhaustion, paranoia and humiliation.

Gathering her things, she pulled her keys from her purse and headed for the front door, using starlight and instinct to guide her along the flagstone-and-white-rock path her father had laid years before.

Nights like this, she missed him more than usual. She'd have talked to him all the way home. He'd have comforted her. Told her she was still a rock star and Owen Matthews had nothing on her.

If only she could hear Dad's voice one more time…

She walked up the porch steps and aimed her keys at the door.

Something crunched on the gravel path behind her. An animal?

A person?

Fear flashed fire to her fingertips. Angie reflexively gripped her keys as she whipped around to face what was likely a protestor who hadn't listened to the warnings the sheriff had doled out. She let the shot of adrenaline fuel her anger. "This is trespassing and I *will* call law enforcement. Leave now."

But the words died as she caught sight of a man at the foot of her porch stairs, not six feet away.

Angie's jaw tightened.

It was tough to make out more than a vague shape in the black night. The man was wearing jeans and a dark hooded sweatshirt zipped to his neck. Something covered the lower half of his face, and his hood was pulled down nearly to his eyes.

He was formless. Shapeless. A living monster.

Angie couldn't move. Couldn't breathe.

This wasn't happening. Regular people didn't find themselves in situations like this. It was the stuff of horror movies.

The man's head tilted, and he regarded her as he walked slowly to the porch, blocking her exit down the stairs. He seemed to size her up, then made his way up the steps methodically, one menacing inch at a time, obviously aware she had nowhere to run, no time to enter the house and bolt herself inside.

No one close enough to hear if she screamed.

Not that she could make a sound. A shriek stuck in her throat, and leaked out as a pathetic whimper. The breath seemed to freeze in her lungs.

Her phone slipped from her fingers and clattered to the wooden porch.

Lights danced in her vision. She might pass out before he reached her. *Jesus, help.* There was no one else. Nothing else. No other salvation.

The figure planted a booted foot on the top step and lifted his hands toward her, seeming to hesitate as though he might be taking pleasure in her fear.

The pause kicked her flight response into gear.

Driven by instinct, Angie charged, shoving all of her weight against the man's chest.

He stumbled backward. His foot hit the edge of the porch at

an awkward angle and he hurtled to the ground, landing hard on his hip. He grunted and cursed as he scrambled up.

Angie didn't wait to see what he did next. She lunged for the door, blindly aiming her keys for the lock.

The porch shook as the man thundered toward her. The key slid into the lock and she turned it.

Strong arms wrapped around her waist and jerked her backward, dragging her away from the door.

A guttural scream escaped her throat and echoed off the trees.

She tried to fight, but he was too strong. He held her too tightly against him.

She couldn't escape.

He dragged her down the stairs, away from her home. Away from safety.

And into a nightmare.

The headlights of National Park Service Investigator Lincoln Tucker's pickup truck swept the front of the two-story white farmhouse at Fairweather Ranch…

And his heart nearly stopped.

At the foot of the steps to the wraparound porch, a man was dragging Angie Garcia toward the side of the house.

As the lights washed over him, the man looked up. A mask covered the lower half of his face. A hood shadowed his eyes. He tightened his grip on Angie.

This was not about to happen. Not on Linc's watch. Not to Angie.

After drawing his sidearm, Linc shoved the door open and jumped out of the truck, holding the pistol low as he stepped forward. "Stop! Federal agent!"

The dark figure froze.

With a fierce scream, Angie drove her foot back and swept the man's leg from under him.

They tumbled to the ground in a heap.

Angie rolled to the side and scrambled to her feet, standing over the figure as though she was going to fight for her life.

"Angie! Back away!" The closer she was to her assailant, the more she risked injury.

Angie eased toward the porch.

When he was about fifteen feet away, Linc stopped and raised his SIG toward the man's center mass as he lay on his back. "Federal agent. Get on your stomach and lace your fingers behind your head."

For a second, the scene froze as though someone had hit the pause button. The only sound was Linc's breathing, short and quick. The next few seconds could change all of their lives. Everything hinged on what the dark stranger did next.

Slowly, the man rolled onto his side, seeming to comply. At the last instant, he jumped to his feet and ran for the corner of the house.

Linc bit back anger and holstered his SIG. Keeping his hand on the grip, he chased the assailant around the corner but stuttered to a halt.

The inky night offered no light. As his eyes adjusted, he could make out trees to his left and the horizon straight ahead, where starry sky met dark ground. On the far side of the narrow stand of trees, an engine started, then a vehicle roared away.

He puffed out his frustration and dragged his hand through his hair, ignoring the way his upper back protested the motion. In a perfect world, he'd call for backup, but by the time they made it to the remote part of the canyon near the Garcia ranch, the suspect would be gone.

"I'm behind you." Angie's voice drifted from the front of the house. Smart of her to warn him she was approaching, especially given the way adrenaline was pumping through his system.

No way would he acknowledge that the sound of her voice gave his heart a different kind of jolt entirely.

When he turned, she was standing about six feet away, highlighted by the glow of his truck's headlights. She was wearing a dressy gray pantsuit, but her feet were bare. Likely she'd lost her shoes in the struggle. Her dark blond hair straggled out of a low bun, evidence of the ordeal she'd been through.

Despite everything, she stood tall, as though someone had rammed a steel rod into her spine.

He tried to read her expression in the shadow across her face. "Are you hurt?" If she was, he'd race after that vehicle himself. On foot. In spite of the pain between his shoulders.

She sniffed and ran her fingers along the hem of her jacket. "He's gone?"

"I heard a vehicle take off, so, yeah, he got away." Saying it made his neck burn with the shame of his weakness and failure. Linc didn't lose his man.

Angie tipped her head and exhaled through pursed lips. "I don't know where he came from. I don't know how he snuck up on me. I don't—"

"It's okay." Linc stepped toward her, recognizing she was rattled and trying to hold it together.

The best thing she could do was fall apart. He'd watched her too many times when Jacob was recovering from the life-altering injuries he'd sustained in combat. Angie had a habit of burying her emotions, tending to the task at hand without letting the pain and fear touch her.

That led to trouble. The kind that made snap decisions.

The kind that ruined friendships and lives.

She held up both hands, building a barrier between them. "I'm fine. I'm not injured. I'm…" She backed away as though Linc was the threat. "I'm fine."

So it was going to be like that. He'd saved her life, and

she was going to act as though he was somehow the villain in her story.

Not that he could blame her. He'd been the one to walk out when she needed him the most, because he couldn't handle—

"Why are you here?" The question was quiet, holding a slight sense of wonder, probably because he'd arrived at the exact right moment. Given that he rarely came to the ranch, his presence there at oh-dark-thirty justified the question. It also kept him from diving too deep into his thoughts about their past.

But before he could answer, he needed to get her somewhere safer than out in the open. If someone genuinely wanted to harm her, a pair of night-vision goggles and a rifle would do the trick. "Let's go inside. We can talk there."

"I…" She turned and walked to the front of the house as though the words had fallen apart before they made it into the air.

Linc trailed her. Yeah, she was definitely working hard to hold it together. It was tough to say if she was succeeding.

On the porch, she scooped up her phone and stared at the door as though she wasn't sure how it worked.

He gathered her shoes from the bottom of the stairs and stepped beside her. "Want me to open it?"

"Do you think it's safe?"

Chances were good. If her assailant had access to the house, he would have waited for her behind closed doors instead of coming at her on the porch. "I'll clear the rooms as soon as we get in. You can wait by the door and get it locked."

"If you're sure."

He nodded. "I'm sure. I'll clear the house, then turn off my truck and we'll talk."

She stepped aside and let him open the door to enter the house first.

He made quick work of checking all of the rooms, then shut

off his truck, made a call to the county sheriff and headed inside.

Angie had turned on all of the lights and was standing in the kitchen on the far side of the island.

No doubt, it was a physical barrier between them, similar to the emotional one he'd built years ago to prevent them from getting too close to one another.

She crossed her arms. "I guess I should thank you."

"No need. I'm glad I was here." He strode across the living room and planted his hands on the island. "You can't do this, Ang."

She straightened and narrowed her eyes. "Do what, Linc?" She hit his name hard, and she loaded it with sarcasm.

The message was clear. He shouldn't have used the familiar nickname her brother used. The one he himself had once affectionately called her.

Too late to retreat now, though. "You can't act like nothing happened, like you're not upset or scared or—"

"Don't tell me how to feel." The walls she'd built were tall. He was quite familiar with them. They resembled his own. "How did you know to be here?"

"Jacob called me."

Her hands fell to her sides with a smack that resounded in the quiet. "How did Jacob know something was wrong? He's in London."

"He tried to call you several times to see how your award thing went, and when you didn't answer, he looked to see where you were." Like a lot of families, Jacob and his wife had linked their devices with Angie's, and they could all see one another's location.

He'd never really understood that.

Of course, he had no one to share information with anyway, so who was he to judge?

"I had my phone on 'do not disturb' for the ceremony and

forgot to switch it." Angie's expression softened. "When Jacob saw I was on the road in the middle of the night—"

"He asked me to check on you. He figured it didn't go well and wanted to make sure you made it home safely. He also gave me strict instructions to tell you to take your phone off DND."

She grabbed the device and thumbed the screen. "Yeah, he called a few times." Glancing up as she set the phone on the counter, she caught his eye. "So did you."

"It's a long drive from Vegas in the middle of the night. I wanted to make sure you were okay." Despite what she thought, he did care about her safety. "And seriously, reactivate your notifications. The sheriff is on the way and he'll need you to open the gate."

"You called the sheriff?" When he nodded, she grabbed the phone, flicked the screen, then slipped it into her pocket. "I'd offer you coffee, but it's so late…"

"I'm good." He slid onto one of the barstools, trying not to wince in pain. He needed to act as though this was just a conversation, but he wanted to get to the bottom of what had happened out there. The quicker they caught the guy, the safer she'd be and the better he'd feel. "Let's talk about what happened."

He glanced around the room. He hadn't been in the main house since Jacob's recovery several years earlier. Any visits he made had been to the cabin Jacob shared with his wife and young daughter about half a mile away. With all of the lights blazing, it was clear three years had changed nothing in the cozy house that bore Angie's touch everywhere he looked.

He shifted on the stool. A detour through the past would get him nowhere in the present.

"I don't want to."

"You need to."

Angie chewed her lower lip and stared at the counter. "What do you think he wanted?"

There was no way to know, but he hoped the light of day would bring answers. Otherwise, the only theory he had was the man had wanted Angie…and it was clear from the boldness of the attack that he would go to any lengths to have her.

TWO

Angie poured two cups of coffee and slid one across the counter to her ranch manager, Rosa Boyd. Thankfully, Rosa had returned that morning, so she'd no longer be alone on the ranch.

She tightened her grip on the coffeepot. She wasn't a fan of the way her hand shook as she settled the carafe onto the burner.

"That's a nice tremor you've got." Naturally, Rosa noticed. Not much got by her. It was one of the reasons Angie had hired her nearly four years earlier. Rosa saw things others missed, whether in people or in the two dozen head of cattle that ranged the land.

When Angie turned, Rosa was watching over the rim of her mug as she took a sip of black coffee.

Plain coffee was something Angie had never understood. She doctored her brew with creamer while she decided how to respond.

"Stalling?"

"No." Sometimes, Rosa was too intuitive. "I got one hour of sleep. My brain isn't firing on all cylinders."

"And the sheriff is outside collecting evidence from your assault."

"Please don't use that word." It made her insides quake. She wasn't ignorant, but she didn't need to keep hearing about it.

She'd gotten her fill from the detective the night before. *Victim. Assault. Attack.* If she never heard those words again, it would be too soon.

Loaded words made it hard to stay in the logical part of her mind. If she was going to get through this, she couldn't let emotions take the reins. The meteorologist in her was trained in scientific facts and data.

Fear had no place in facts.

Rosa flipped her long, dark braid over her shoulder and said nothing.

No way was Angie falling for that trick. She wasn't filling the silence with words. Instead, she defiantly sipped her coffee. Rosa had been raised on a Colorado ranch and had spent her life outdoors. Though she was only a couple of years older than Angie's thirty-three, her dark skin bore the evidence of wind and sun. She had a ready smile and was incredibly organized. While Angie ran the research center, Rosa had charge of the ranch and the three hands who worked there.

Rosa broke the silence. "I saw Lincoln Tucker when I came in."

Guess even she couldn't stay quiet forever, but it would have been nice if she'd landed on a different topic.

"Jacob sent him to check on me."

"Good thing."

That was the other fact Angie hadn't wanted to acknowledge. If Lincoln hadn't pulled into the driveway when he did…

Her stomach turned in on itself. She shoved aside her coffee, the brew suddenly acidic.

"So this *does* bother you." Deep furrows creased Rosa's forehead. "You can't do the thing where you act like nothing's wrong."

"I already got a speech from Linc. And I'm fine."

"Then why did you turn so pale?" Rosa snapped her fingers. "That fast. When I mentioned Linc."

"Stop." Angie dumped her coffee in the sink, then opened the fridge. Yogurt would make her stomach feel less like it was practicing gymnastics, wouldn't it? After snagging a container of peach, she shut the door. "Fill me in on the ranch." Regardless of what had happened the night before, they had a business to run. Their morning meetings were meant to be a rundown of the day, not an airing of personal business.

With a sigh, Rosa pulled her phone from her hip pocket and flicked the screen. "Wiley and Danny are back from their nights off and will inspect the fence line today. Ellis rode out yesterday morning with the cattle. He'll be back this evening. We have a couple of head in the barn waiting on a scheduled vet check this afternoon. Also, Carter Holbert called. There was an issue with his renovation at the Desert View Watchtower, so he may not get here today to finish the demo on the old cabins where we're building the second dormitory."

"Just as well. There's too much happening here anyway." She also needed to find the money now that she'd lost the grant she'd been counting on. She could dig into savings, but the thought of losing her cushion made her stomach quake.

She shoved her spoon into her half-eaten yogurt and set it aside.

"Let's talk about Carter, since he needs to be paid." Naturally, Rosa followed her thoughts. "How did the award go last night?"

"It didn't."

Rosa's expression dropped. "I was sure you were a slam dunk."

Same. Angie stared past Rosa at the front window as Detective Kari Blankenship passed, studying the wide porch boards.

Between the loss and the…incident, it was no wonder food wasn't Angie's friend this morning.

"Who won?"

"I'd rather not say."

"Not Crucial Causes."

"Don't make it sound like we wanted another group to lose." Although if *she* had to lose, why did it have to be to the organization Owen Matthews chaired?

"That's why you came back last night instead of staying for the rest of the conference."

Rosa was one of the few who knew the whole story about her history with Owen, the man she was supposed to marry. The one she'd dated junior and senior years in college. The one who'd made her so many promises that she'd lost count.

The one who'd eloped with his old high-school girlfriend over spring break, two months before graduation.

The betrayal had shattered Angie's trust and reset her future. The moment her roommate had shown her the social-media post of Owen's last-minute Vegas wedding, Angie had denied it, then grown angry... Then had been intent on not letting him see he'd wrecked her.

She'd set aside her pain and thrown herself into finals, refusing to hear apologies or excuses. They'd both been in the running for the Johnson-Markly Scholarship to fund their graduate studies in meteorology, and she'd been determined to win.

She had.

She'd been equally determined to succeed at everything she'd attempted since, to prove to Owen that he hadn't beaten her down. Grant after grant, award after award, she'd outpaced him.

Until last night, when she'd sat across from him for the first time since college at a ceremony for the largest grant she'd ever pursued. Half a million dollars would have funded the new dormitory and research center she wanted to add to the existing buildings on the property.

She'd lost to Owen. Publicly. In front of hundreds of their colleagues.

Her research facility was in jeopardy, and her pride had taken an intense blow.

Adding insult to injury, Lincoln was outside her front door, another reminder of her horrible past judgment. *God, did You really have to bring every humiliation at once?*

"Let me guess." Rosa stood and reached for her hat, which she'd laid on a barstool. "You don't want to talk about the grant, either?"

"Not especially."

"Let's circle back to Lincoln."

Definitely not. That part of her history was the one thing Rosa didn't know.

No one did. Not even Jacob knew what had happened to wreck their friendship. "I do not want to talk about Lincoln."

The front door opened and the man himself stepped through, holding a small paper bag. "Did I hear my name?"

Rosa planted her brown Stetson on her head and turned her back to Linc, dropping a wink at Angie. "Not that I heard." With a wave, she headed for the side door. "I have to get to the ranch. I'll check on the researchers and tell them you'll be over later."

"Thanks." There were currently four researchers-in-residence on the property. Two meteorologists and two archaeologists were studying the effects of weather on artifacts in the canyon in an effort to develop better preservation techniques.

When the door closed behind Rosa, Lincoln stepped into the living room. Shadows under his blue eyes told of his sleepless night aiding the sheriff's department in their investigation. His light brown hair looked as though he'd run his hands through it, a nervous habit Angie recognized. He'd slid the top back until it was nearly flat, though the short sides remained styled. His close-shaven beard needed a trim. In dark cargo pants and a gray polo, he looked the part of a federal agent.

An *exhausted* federal agent.

No matter how uncomfortable their relationship was, she owed him her life. The least she could do was offer him breakfast. "You hungry?"

"That's why I came in." He strode across the room as though he lived there and settled the bag on the counter. "I had one of the guys on the team bring breakfast burritos from Misty's."

Misty's was a tiny lunch counter in the back of a gas station/general store only locals really knew about. Misty made some of the best eats in Arizona.

Suddenly, her stomach felt like it could handle food.

Linc opened the bag but paused to glance at his phone. He frowned.

"Do you need to get that?"

"No." He pocketed the device and passed a paper-wrapped bundle across the counter. "I'll trade you for coffee."

"Deal." Angie poured the cup and handed it over, then bit into the flour tortilla wrapped around the burrito. Spicy sausage and fiery homemade salsa were tempered by egg and melted cheese.

It was exactly what she needed.

Linc chased a healthy bite with coffee. "I remembered how much you liked them from when…" He set his cup on the table. Uncertainty hazed his normally confident demeanor. "I remembered you liked them."

Without looking at him, Angie bit into her own burrito, although she'd lost her appetite again. He remembered from their time tagteaming during Jacob's recovery, helping him through the mental, physical and emotional issues he'd wrestled with when an IED had scrambled his insides and nearly killed him.

When her own emotions had overflowed in the trauma and had sought an outlet…

As had Lincoln's.

Then, she'd been a different person. Scared. Angry. Lost. She'd been—

Her phone trilled with three quick rings that indicated a call from Rosa. She'd take anything to derail her train of thought. She pulled the phone to her ear. "Hey, what's—"

"You need to get down here with the sheriff." Rosa was breathless. "We were hit by vandals again."

He probably ought to be thankful the phone had rung when it had. They'd been two seconds from a conversation he wasn't ready to have. The night he'd walked out of this house had been tough on both of them. The more time that passed, the more awkward it was to discuss.

Even so, news about more trouble on the ranch wasn't the distraction he'd have chosen.

Neither was that call from his doctor. He was supposed to be at the hospital right now, getting the MRI that might clear him to return to full duty. The fall he'd taken a couple of weeks earlier in training had sidelined him, and today was the day he was supposed to find out how soon he'd get his life back. Hopefully, they'd skip surgery and go the route of pain meds and physical therapy, but he'd put in the work no matter what they said.

Right now, though, he had more pressing things to deal with.

Given the way Angie was working the hem of her sweat-shirt through her fingers as he started the pickup, she was feeling the effects of everything coming at her. What had happened to Angie was a traumatic event, and she needed to process the ramifications.

Knowing her, though, she was wielding a heavy-duty shovel and trying to bury it, which was the worst thing she could do.

"Linc?" Her voice was small, which was unlike her. Not even two minutes earlier, she'd demanded to ride along, not giving him any room to say no.

That was Angie. She tended to charge in and take control.

She handled what needed to be handled, sometimes to her detriment. She was competitive and driven to win.

Hearing her quiet tone twisted his gut.

Especially since he knew part of her problem was this guy, right here, behind the steering wheel. "Yeah?"

"Did you guys get any clues to who was at the house last night?"

"Not a thing." He hated telling her. All he'd wanted was to find some condemning piece of evidence that would point them straight to her attacker.

Instead, they had nothing. Not even a usable shoe print. Even the clearing beyond the woods, where the assailant had escaped, hadn't yielded any clues, just indistinguishable tire tracks on the pine needles heading toward the canyon and the back entrance to the ranch.

Angie looked straight out the front window. She was diving into her head, and he needed to pull her into the present. When she withdrew, she tended to stay locked away from her emotions for days, weeks…or longer.

He sifted through a few thoughts, then hit upon the one least likely to spark an uncomfortable conversation. "Hey, can you clarify a few things? I want the facts straight in my head so I don't overlook something important."

"I guess. Yeah." It wasn't the most enthusiastic response, but it was something.

Linc pulled out of the drive and aimed the truck for the ranch, taking the old asphalt road at a slower pace than usual to give Angie time to talk.

"Let's think about the protestors, since they've caused some trouble on the property recently. I heard you tell Detective Blankenship you're friends with some of them?" If he was going to guess, he'd say the trouble started with the group that had been gathering outside the gate for several weeks.

"One of them. Monica Huerta and I went to school together

and now we go to church together, but we're more acquaintances than friends."

"When's the last time you two spoke?"

"Nearly two weeks ago at church, the Sunday before I headed to Vegas. She told me they'd figured out who vandalized a couple of the old cabins last week, the ones we'd slated to tear down. Detective Blankenship told me this morning the names of the trespassers had been turned over to the county, and I have the option to prosecute."

He was certain the county would check alibis for the whereabouts of those two for the previous night, but he'd ask to be sure. "So will you press charges?" It would send a message to anyone else thinking of causing trouble for her.

"I don't know. They broke a couple of windows and spray-painted on the walls. They really didn't hurt anything."

"They trespassed. That's a way bigger issue." If the protestors felt they had a right to be on Angie's property, then they might be emboldened to try far worse crimes than tagging a couple of old structures.

Crimes like assault…or kidnapping.

"If you're thinking that's who came at me, I doubt it. No one has even so much as raised their voice at me or anyone else as we've passed the gate."

Trespassing and vandalism were a far cry from "raised voices," but it seemed Angie was determined to stay in denial. "Why do the protestors want to shut you down?"

She turned from the window to give him a withering look. "Jacob's your best friend. You're not ignorant about what I want to do here."

At least she was feeling some emotion, although he'd prefer it wasn't animosity toward him. There was still something ugly sitting between them. A couple of years ago, when he'd been helping Jacob protect the woman who was now his wife, Ivy, and their daughter, Wren, Linc had spent a little bit of time with Angie as they kept the kid out of harm's way. It had been an uneasy, short-lived truce, but she'd filled him in on some of her plans for her family's property. Still, having her tell him again would ground him in the story and might help him discover a clue. It would also keep her from holding everything in. "Humor me."

With a heavy sigh, she stared out the front windshield. "In the 1850s, my several-times-over great-grandfather purchased this land and built the cabin where Jacob lives. This was before the National Park Service was a thing. He brought in cattle and started ranching. When the government started creating Grand Canyon National Park in the early 1900s, the family opted not to sell."

Their situation wasn't unusual. The country's national parks were dotted with private land, "inholdings" that had been in families for generations. Most of the time they went unnoticed, but there were instances when frustrations about private land in public parks boiled over. "So the protestors want you to, what? Walk away?"

"They want me to cease constructing and running the research center and to hand the land over to the government. They see what I'm doing as development and not as conservation or research. Somehow, they've gotten the idea all of this will operate as a resort."

"When that's the furthest thing from what you're intending."

"Right. I want to preserve what's here and to make sure the canyon is cared for long after we're gone. A private research facility will help. If I walk away, I can't control what happens, and I want to know the land is being used for the best purposes. Initially, this was about meteorological research, but I realized we could do more good if I modeled us after the North Rim ranches, which are working ranches with small herds, research facilities and conservation areas. There are scientists coming in to study everything from climate to plants and animals to the land itself. I'm providing a place for them to work and live while they're here. The plan is to offer an inexpensive alternative to researchers who can't get the grants they need." She bit off the words at the end, almost bitterly.

Interesting, but no time to chase that rabbit down the trail now. "So you're actually doing what they want, but they can't see that because you're not doing it their way."

"Maybe? I think they believe the government can do a better job. Maybe they can. But there are bigger things I want to do. We're just beginning. We'll be a dedicated space that isn't funded by tax dollars." She waved a hand in the air. "I know it's what I'm supposed to do, if that makes sense."

Like he knew he belonged in the canyon and not sitting behind a desk. "And the cultural part?"

"So much has happened with the eleven tribes who have lived here for longer than we've been a country. Weather affects them. Tourism affects them. Government policies affect them. There are ways to get permission to dig in the park to maintain and preserve artifacts. Rosa and I started thinking… What if we provided a place to act as home base for the tribes and those working with them, so they can further preserve their history and culture? It goes along with what I'm already doing, and it's really my passion project. More than the weather side of it, which shocked me since that's what my degree is in."

"I get it." The tribes around the canyon had long struggled, and that was part of the reason he was passionate about his own job.

Linc would have said more, but they were approaching the ranch. As he turned to make his way across the cattle guard in the road, he scanned the area. Beyond the massive horse barn that the ranch horses were housed in, construction equipment waited to be used. It was clear that work hadn't started for the day and had possibly been halted due to the presence of law enforcement. Several debris piles stood nearby. "Is that what's left of the vandalized cabins?"

Angie followed his gaze. "Yeah."

"What did they paint on the buildings?"

She puffed out a breath. "Same as the signs out by the gate. 'Stop destroying the land' and 'no more tourists.' Oh, and 'the Canyon belongs to everyone.' As if one person could own it. We don't even back up to the canyon. There are several miles between us and the rim. The sheriff thinks the vandals got in by cutting across public land and coming through one of our back gates."

It was also the likely ingress and egress point for her attacker. "You should have cameras on those."

"Or the ranch workers and I should start coming in that way so the protestors don't know when we're here."

Hiding wasn't like Angie. His heart hurt for her. It couldn't be easy to be the target of a group who misunderstood and opposed you. "How long has this been going on?"

"They started camping out here when I pulled the permits to build a bunkhouse and a second research facility about three weeks ago. I guess the idea of two new buildings was more than someone could bear."

Possibly. But that man hadn't been simply trying to stop her—he'd been trying to take her, and maybe worse.

Linc feared it *was* worse, and the issue with her land was something they hadn't considered. Something someone out there was willing to kill for.

THREE

As Linc slowed to a stop behind two sheriff's SUVs near the cabins, Angie tapped her knee, wishing she could be anywhere else. Had her week gone the way she'd planned, she'd have awakened in Vegas this morning, hit an enormous breakfast buffet and would have been sitting in on group discussions about weather and the environment.

Instead, she was stuck in a pickup truck with the only man aside from Owen who'd ever left scars on her heart. The one man whose presence reminded her of her weakest moment, one he'd had to deflect and one she could never forget. Shame burned far too often.

It was no wonder Linc had essentially avoided her since.

Which begged the question… "Linc, why are you here?" He could have left. Her case was for the sheriff's department, not for the level of Linc's federal investigative team. As far as any obligation to her was concerned, he was finished once the deputies arrived.

"I'm here because Jacob asked me to be."

Of course. The two of them were as close as brothers, although the tension between Linc and Angie meant she rarely saw them together. Jacob could be overprotective, but how many guys could say the love of their lives had been targeted by a hired killer? Still, her brother had other friends he could have called.

"But why you specifically?" Linc was happier scaling canyon walls and hiking isolated areas. He thrived on seeking evidence in the toughest, most remote places in the park.

While he claimed this was about Jacob, there had to be more. Why was he cooling his heels on her ranch?

Something Jacob had mentioned recently tweaked at a memory, but it didn't hold. He rarely talked to her about Lincoln, although they had been battle buddies in the army, until Linc decided to become an investigator for the National Park Service. After Jacob suffered massive internal injuries overseas, Linc had convinced him to make a career with the NPS.

That move had probably saved her brother's life.

"He asked me because I'm available." His voice was husky, heavy with a timbre that could make a girl's stomach quake.

If she was that kind of girl. And if he wasn't Lincoln Tucker. Linc wasn't a guy who wanted commitment. He'd made that abundantly clear the night she'd destroyed their friendship.

It had happened at the end of a grueling thirty-six hours during Jacob's recovery, and they'd both been up all day, all night and through another day, walking him through the pain. Exhausted, all of her filters had worn away. In the fog of fatigue and emotion, she'd essentially thrown herself at Lincoln.

He'd nearly caught her.

While she was grateful he'd set the brake, her humiliation had built a wall between them. Their friendship had fallen apart. He'd no longer been by her side in nursing Jacob. Instead, he'd switched off duties with her, taking the nights so she could sleep, then disappearing during the days. Clearly, he'd been wary of being alone with her.

Things hadn't been easy between them since. He was uneasy around her. She was angry and hurt by his rejection, then ultimately embarrassed by her behavior. The more time that passed, the harder it was to address the moment.

And the more time they spent apart, the harder it was to be in his presence.

It hadn't been long after when Rosa had come to the house and witnessed a rare emotional breakdown. When Rosa had prayed her through it, Angie had realized what it meant that Jesus loved her. Everything changed…

Except the gulf between Lincoln and herself. Some days, she missed their friendship. Others, he reminded her of her own weaknesses, of the road she'd nearly traveled in a search for acceptance and love.

She cleared her throat of rising shame. "You're a team leader. Doesn't your team need you?"

Lincoln's grip on the wheel tightened. "Angie, listen. There are a lot of things at play." He killed the engine and turned his entire body to face her. It wasn't the first time he'd moved as though his neck and shoulders were fused. "The best thing we can do is keep this professional. I'm here because Jacob asked me to be here. Anything else is…" Abruptly, he pushed open the door and stared toward the nearest cabin, where Detective Blankenship was speaking with Rosa and a man she didn't recognize. "Anything else is something we'll discuss on any day other than this one." The truck rocked when he got out and slammed the door.

Big talk from a guy who'd been all up in her business a few minutes earlier.

Still, he was right. There was no need for a personal discussion. Ever. They'd done fine keeping their distance, and it was best to maintain the status quo.

Her heart couldn't handle any other option.

She'd tuck him away in the logical lockbox where she'd kept his memory for three years. No emotion was allowed there.

Stepping out of the truck, she slid on sunglasses against the early morning sun. This day had been too long already, and it was only a few minutes after nine.

Ignoring the official vehicles, she scanned the area. On the edge of the Kaibab National Forest, patches of trees dotted the red landscape that stretched to the canyon's rim several miles away. To the right of the five employee cabins, where they'd parked, a fence outlined a corral by a large barn that housed the ranch horses. Beyond, a dormitory provided space for six guest researchers.

To the left of the wide main path, a larger cabin housed the ranch's office and Rosa's living quarters.

Beside it stood the building that made her chest swell with professional pride. Built to blend with the older cabins, the research center was four thousand square feet of office and laboratory space. Half a dozen researchers worked in the center at a time, but they'd recently broken ground on the second dormitory and a research facility behind the barn.

Her dream wavered in her stomach. For a few hours, the previous night's grant loss had been overshadowed by the fear she'd been wrestling down. Now burning humiliation rose. She'd been counting on the grant to carry her through construction. Without it, the expansion would take all of her savings, and the thought of operating without a safety net paralyzed her.

Not only had she lost to Owen, but protestors also wanted her to fail.

And someone might be willing to harm her in order to put an end to her dream.

A wave of nausea made the horizon seem as if it was wobbling. She pressed her hand against the warm hood of Linc's truck and waited for the wave to crest. When she closed her eyes, her mind played the movie of that man, creeping up the steps…

With a gasp, she opened her eyes. *Deep breaths. Clean air.* She forced the image away. The man was gone. She was safe. *Maybe.*

Forcing herself into the present, she followed Linc as he approached the small group of people standing in front of Ellis West's cabin. The two side windows were broken, but there was none of the graffiti she'd expected.

When another wave of anxiety threatened, she willed her brain into thoughts over feelings. *One crisis at a time. Handle what you can fix.* This was a time for action, not for emotion.

Rosa broke away from her conversation with Detective Blankenship and the stranger who was wearing a deputy's uniform, perhaps Blankenship's partner.

The site of Rosa's familiar braid and cowboy hat calmed Angie's nerves. They'd gotten through a lot while working together, and they'd get through this as well.

The law-enforcement officers ended their discussion, and the man stepped forward, extending his hand. "I'm Detective Blankenship's partner, Duane Majenty." His dark hair was cropped short, and his brown eyes scanned her face. "How are you doing, Ms. Garcia?"

Behind him, Linc watched the proceedings, but he said nothing.

Angie kept her attention on the younger detective. "I'm fine. What happened?" If she focused on one thing at a time, she might get through this day.

Before he could respond, Detective Blankenship stepped beside him. "Ms. Garcia, I need your permission to enter the cabin."

Angie looked over the other woman's shoulder at Rosa. "Didn't Ellis take the satellite phone? Call him. He can give you permission." While she owned the property, she wasn't comfortable allowing someone into Ellis's space without his consent.

"I haven't been able to reach him." Rosa eased to the side so she could speak around Blankenship. "I've tried several times but it doesn't connect."

The ranch maintained a small herd, largely to study the effects of sustainable livestock practices on land overgrazed in the past. When the hands were out with the cattle, they kept in contact by satellite phone. It wasn't unusual for them to be unreachable for brief periods due to sunspots, weather or terrain.

The day was clear, however, and the area where Ellis was working was wide open.

"I'd prefer not to wait," Detective Blankenship said. "As the owner of the property, you can give us permission."

"I thought this was vandalism. It's the exterior that's the problem." Her eyes went to Linc in silent question.

"On initial thought, yes, but…" He puffed air out, then turned her gently toward the broken windows. "Look again."

Angie tried to see what Lincoln saw. The lack of graffiti. The busted windows. The glass on the ground glinting in the—

The glass. If someone had vandalized Ellis's cabin by breaking the windows, the glass would largely be inside the structure.

She grabbed Linc's forearm.

Whoever had broken those windows had done the damage from the inside.

This wasn't vandalism.

It was something much worse.

Linc took a wide berth around the side of the cabin, making sure not to step on any glass. He stopped and studied the window. Because the cabin was raised to allow air to flow underneath, the windows were high enough he couldn't see inside.

He scanned the broken panes and the glass on the ground, searching for evidence of blood but finding none. At least he could partially rule out someone being shoved through the window. Still, the observation left him with more questions than answers.

Answers they'd only find inside the silent structure.

Beside him, Detective Majenty had kneeled to photograph

the glass. He looked to the front of the building, where Angie was with Blankenship and the ranch manager, then stood so he was shoulder to shoulder with Linc. "What do you think we're going to find inside?" He kept his voice low, probably to keep Angie from hearing.

Good call. She'd been through enough. The way she was tugging at the sleeves on her shirt spoke to the stress she was trying to tamp down. If he hadn't been so self-focused years ago, he might be able to offer her some comfort now. Instead, she'd reject him if he tried. Rightly so.

He kneaded the dull pain in his neck, ignoring the way his fingers tingled. He'd have to call the doc when he had a minute and reschedule that MRI. It was the only shot he had of getting cleared to go back out.

Of being useful again.

"Agent Tucker?" The detective was waiting for an answer.

"Yeah. Right. I'm not sure, but it's possible there'll be signs of a struggle. I doubt anyone would *intentionally* break a window from the inside for no reason." Linc motioned for Majenty to follow him to the rear of the building. "You guys check the perimeter yet?"

"No. We saw the damage to the window, knew it was from the interior and called you. Blankenship has decided, this close to the park, she wants to keep you looped in. The protestors make her squirrelly. She's put in a request for you to act as a liaison between your agency and the sheriff's department."

At the corner of the cabin, Linc stopped and looked at the detective. "Sounds like a plan. Until the official word comes through, I'm here as an advisor."

"Appreciate it."

He stopped to tug on his gloves as Majenty did the same. "The main thing I want to know once we've determined what happened is how this links to the attack at the main house. There's no way this is a coincidence."

There were so many other questions as well. If Ellis was out on the ranch land, who had been in his cabin? Was Ellis truly out of sat-phone range, or had something terrible happened?

Only one way to find out. "Let's do this." Linc rounded the corner and headed for the back door, but he stopped with his foot on the bottom step of the stoop.

Using a key Rosa had provided, Linc unlocked the door and eased it open. He stepped into a small entry that held a stacked washer and dryer and a wooden bench. He paused to listen as Majenty stepped into the space behind him. Only the low hum of the refrigerator in the kitchen marred the silence.

From Rosa's description, he knew the small kitchen came next, with a bedroom and connecting bathroom to the right. On the other side of the kitchen would be an open living area.

That's where the busted windows were. He stepped into the kitchen and aimed at the bedroom with two fingers, directing Majenty to clear the room.

The kitchen was spotless, but several clods of red dirt, likely from the treads of a shoe, lay in a path along the floor to the living area.

He sniffed the air, praying it wouldn't reveal the metallic scent of blood.

It didn't. Just the vague smell of bacon.

He stepped into the living area and scanned it. No closets. No place to hide. The room was empty. "Clear." Holstering his weapon, he surveyed the space.

Majenty echoed him and entered the kitchen. "Bedroom's clear also. Not a sign of anything out of place."

"I wish I could say the same." He motioned Majenty forward.

It was obvious there had been a struggle. An oval coffee table was turned on its side and had been shoved against the wood-framed couch. A barstool from the counter that divided living room from kitchen was splintered near the window, possibly the weapon that had shattered the glass. Blood was smeared along several of the stool's wooden shards and had spattered across the floor.

Linc kneeled and studied the trail. It wasn't enough blood for someone to bleed out, but it was enough to indicate an injury, almost as though the victim had taken a blow to the nose or mouth. "Definitely was a fight in here. How did no one hear the struggle or the glass breaking?"

Majenty paused in photographing the space. "Rosa was gone last night, and she said the ranch hands on both sides were away as well. The one immediately next door went to visit his family for a birthday party and didn't get back until late. The other went to visit his girlfriend, but he stays two cabins away. Both rode out before dawn this morning to check perimeter fences. The other two cabins are empty in preparation for renovation."

Whoever did this had to know there was little possibility they'd be heard, which indicated they'd either been watching the cabins, or they knew the movements of the workers and guests.

"Let's try to get DNA from the blood, see if it belongs to Ellis or to someone else." Hopefully, they'd get a hit in a database.

Linc walked to the kitchen counter, where a stack of mail rested. "I'm not liking how this looks. If Ellis is out with the cattle, who was here?"

"Maybe he came back to meet someone? That doesn't track, either, though. Rosa said his horse isn't in the barn, so he's likely still out."

It simply didn't make sense. Linc filtered through the stack of opened envelopes, but it offered no clues. A generic postcard of the canyon with no message, just signed with a heart by someone named Nica, a campaign ad and a credit-card statement that revealed nothing out of the ordinary.

He set down the mail, then walked to the front door and pulled it open. Stepping onto the small porch, he avoided looking at Angie, who hesitated at the foot of the stairs.

He couldn't face her, not when he had no answers to the storm brewing around her. Instead, he turned to Rosa. "Do me a favor. Call Ellis's sat phone again."

"Is he…?" Angie widened her stance as though she expected a blow. "Is he in there?"

Linc shook his head. No need to give her the details of what they'd found, especially given it made no sense.

Rosa dialed and listened, then shook her head and pocketed her cell. "Nothing."

"Okay, here's another question." Linc jerked his thumb over his shoulder. "Did you happen to walk by the cabin yesterday? Are you sure the window wasn't broken before last night?" Maybe something had happened to Ellis before he was supposed to ride out. Their timeline could be flawed.

Rosa scanned the sky as though searching for something, then slowly shook her head. "No, it wasn't broken before. I was at Danny's next door yesterday, talking to him before he left. I'd have noticed the glass."

"There's a geolocator on Ellis's sat phone, so we need to look into that." If the device was getting even a weak signal, they could ping it and figure out if he was actually out on the ranch, where he was supposed to be. "And you're sure he left?"

"I'm certain. I helped him gear up yesterday morning. Some of our guys ride ATVs, but Ellis is old-school. He might be young, but he likes being out on his horse. Chance is not in the stable. I fed the horses about an hour ago and he's the only one gone." Rosa backed a few steps toward her cabin. "I have a program on the office computer that can ping the phone."

Detective Blankenship looked up from her cell. "I'll go with her."

When Angie didn't move, Linc jerked his head toward the women. "You go, too."

"Not until you tell me what's in the cabin. I own the place. I have a right to know."

Ah, there she was. This was the Angie he was used to. Stubborn. Defiant. Bossy to her own detriment.

He nearly smiled, but the situation weighed too heavily. "Nothing. Looks like a fight went down in there. Not sure what to make of it. And, no, you can't come in. It's a crime scene." He texted Thomas Canady, who was acting as team leader while Linc healed. Do what it takes to get us assigned to an assault and a possible missing person on Fairweather Ranch. Send a crime-scene unit to my location.

The reply was immediate. I'll get the necessary permissions. Shouldn't be hard since it's an inholding within the park. Might take time. Hearing rumors of another case coming our way. Will update you later. Need anything else?

No. Coconino County was capable of investigating, but he wanted the added power behind his own team. The sheriff's department didn't have all of the resources his federal team did.

But what else would his team be investigating that he hadn't heard about? His fingers itched to ask for details, but he needed to focus on what was happening in front of him.

He walked down the stairs to Angie. "I want to get you to the house. We'll let these guys do their job and—"

"Agent Tucker!" Detective Blankenship burst out the door to the office at a full run, headed for the stables. "We got a hit on the sat phone."

Linc glanced at Angie. "Stay here." He jogged after the detective, who stopped at the back of the barn and started scanning the ground.

She pointed toward the corner of the building, her expression grim. "There."

Half-hidden in a bale of hay, a phone was barely visible.

Someone had clearly shoved it there, likely in an attempt to hide it in a hurry.

Lincoln balled his fists and stared toward the horizon. Ellis West wasn't out on the ranch with the cattle. He'd come back, likely the night before. Was he responsible for what had happened to Angie? "Let's wait until—"

A gunshot cracked.

Linc whirled toward the sound as the firearm's echo mingled with Angie's scream.

FOUR

Angie bit back another scream as Detective Majenty shoved her toward the porch steps of Ellis's cabin.

He dragged Rosa along beside him and moved her in front of him, urging her to follow Angie. "Get inside. Go to the left. Stay low." The detective drew his pistol as he pushed her onto the porch, staring in the direction of the gunshot's echo.

Another crack sounded across the distance, and wood splintered on the corner of Rosa's cabin.

The two women scrambled through the front door and dropped into the corner beneath the window on the left, then huddled together in the small space.

Angie struggled to catch her breath. The world was moving too fast, seeming to spin triple-time on its axis. Surely she was living in a horrible dream or in the rising action of a horror movie. The world seemed unreal—exactly the same as it had the night before, when that man approached her.

"What in the world?" Rosa's voice was hot, blazing with anger. She shifted as though she planned to stand and charge outside. "If I had my rifle—"

"You'd stay right here." Angie grabbed her friend's arm and dragged her to the floor beside her. Both of them needed to get their minds into gear. Rosa needed to withdraw from action mode. Angie needed to settle into it. She couldn't afford to devolve into a puddled mess of fear any more than

Rosa could afford to charge out into the unknown with literal and metaphorical guns blazing. "We need to let the authorities handle this."

Rosa made a face and settled against the wall, her expression tight. It was killing her to sit still when she could be helping.

Well, it might kill her to step into the fray.

Angie closed her eyes and counted to ten, inhaling the faint smell of bacon that permeated Ellis's cabin, grounding herself in the moment. Everything had fallen silent outside, and the only sound was Rosa's breathing and the light hum of something in the cabin. She focused on scents and sounds, trying to shove aside how someone had fired two shots at them.

Someone had tried to kill them.

She gasped, then struggled to wrestle her breathing into rhythm. She would not panic. Could not panic. This was her ranch. She was in charge. Falling apart in a moment of weakness would serve no one.

Falling apart in a moment of weakness always led to trouble. Always.

Beside her, Rosa shifted. "You okay?"

Angie took three more deep breaths, then nodded. "We're safe in here. The walls in these cabins are old, heavy timber. It would take a tank to blast through one of them." Hopefully, there were none of those rolling toward them.

"You saying that to convince me or to convince yourself?"

Angie shot her what she hoped was a cutting look. "Don't."

"Don't what?"

"Don't pick a fight with me so you don't have to think about what's happening outside." She tilted her head, listening. Someone was on the porch, likely Detective Majenty keeping an eye on the front door.

There was a back door to the cabin as well. Who was guarding that?

She shook off the thought. No need to invent imaginary

monsters at the gate when there were very real ones already stalking the ranch. Angie fought a shudder and focused on the tension radiating off Rosa.

"Oh, don't pick a fight with you? How about you don't sit over there and force your brain into a place where nothing is wrong so you don't have to deal with reality?" Rosa pivoted to face her. "Fear is a real emotion, you know. And an under-standable one."

Angie dug her teeth into her bottom lip to keep from saying something she'd regret later. "Back at you." The words were ground out in frustration and anger and, yes, fear.

Rosa smirked. "I'm not denying I'm terrified. I'm masking it with rage."

Outside, a female voice rang between the cabins. "All clear!" It sounded like Detective Blankenship.

From the rear of the cabin, Linc's voice answered. "Clear here!"

Angie sank against the wall and closed her eyes again. They were safe, for now. Linc was safe for now. She hadn't let her-self acknowledge he was out there in the open with whoever was shooting at them, but she couldn't deny the weakness of relief at the sound of his voice.

Beside her, Rosa mimicked her posture, bending her knees and propping her elbows on them. "Neither of us handles being out of control well, I guess."

Angie leaned her shoulder against Rosa's. "Never have."

"We've been through a lot together, but being shot at is a new one."

Angie opened her eyes and stared into the kitchen. She'd rather forget it had happened. Talking solidified the threat in her brain. Made it real. The last thing she wanted was for this moment to sear itself into her memory. She had enough trouble forgetting what had happened the night before. If she could get through the next few minutes, she could survive it and put it into the past.

Unlike last night. A man's hands pulling her away, tugging her toward—

She stood and shook her hands at her sides. "They said it's clear. We need to get moving."

Rosa reached up and grabbed her hand, her head cocked to one side and her ever-present cowboy hat askew. "Ang, seriously. Please don't. It's okay to be—"

"I'm fine. It's over." She pulled her hand from her friend's grasp. Rosa didn't understand. Emotions swamped her. They clouded her judgment. They made her miss the truth about people who could hurt her, and they made her do things she shouldn't. "There's too much happening to deal with this now."

Rosa stood, staring her in the eye. "This *is* now. This *is* happening. If you keep burying the bad, eventually even the good is going to escape you."

"I'm fine." She pulled her gaze away from Rosa's and stared over her friend's shoulder. Her eyes widened. "Rosa…"

What she was seeing couldn't be real. Linc was right. There had been a fight in the cabin. Furniture was broken. The window was shattered. And the floor was smeared with—

"Angie? Rosa?" Linc's voice came from the rear of the house, dragging Angie's gaze from the renewed horror she was viewing. He strode in from the kitchen. "Are you two okay?"

The question skimmed Rosa and landed straight on Angie. His eyes scanned her from head to toe, as though he wanted reassurance that she hadn't been hit.

She turned her gaze to the refrigerator, ignoring the gentle heat his concern created in her stomach. It was taking all of her strength to hold fear at bay. She didn't need whatever this was to come in and crack the dam holding all of her emotions in check.

Rosa responded when it became clear Angie wouldn't.

"We're good. Detective Majenty got us inside quickly. Is everyone outside okay?"

"We're all good." Linc came all the way into the living area, holstering his pistol as he did. "Whoever it was took two shots then fled. We heard the vehicle leave. They were in a stand of trees on the far side of the paddock."

"I'm headed out, then. I want to call Danny and Wiley in, let them know what's going on. They don't need to be out there on ATVs if someone's taking potshots at us."

"Good idea. Keep everyone close. It may be time to consider getting your guests off the ranch until this blows over."

At the suggestion, Angie's head jerked, a sizzle of panic running along her nerves. "No." If the researchers left, then refunds were in order. They couldn't afford to let money go now.

Immediately, guilt cooled her concern. Money could be replaced. Lives couldn't. Linc was right. For the safety of all involved, they needed to clear the researchers from the property. She turned to Rosa. "Go ahead. Let them know what's going on. Tell them we'll hold their spots and keep an eye on what they leave behind if they want to go."

Rosa nodded and headed toward the door.

"Wait." A horrible thought shuddered through her. "Chance. Ellis's horse. Can we get someone looking for him? If he's not in the barn, he's out there somewhere."

Rosa's expression darkened. "I'll make sure Danny and Wiley get out to search immediately."

"I want to talk to them first." Linc looked between the two women. "It's standard procedure. We'll need to check alibis and ask them a few questions."

"Really?" Angie couldn't imagine either Danny or Wiley harming Ellis. The men were like brothers.

Rosa closed her arms, her posture rigid. "You'll want mine, too?"

"Like I said, standard procedure."

With a curt nod, Rosa walked out the door, her head held high as though they hadn't been targets a few minutes earlier.

Linc waited for her to leave before he spoke. "I doubt your people had anything to do with it, but we have to check all of the boxes, so, please, don't fuss at me."

Angie swallowed her next words. Her brother was on Linc's team. She well knew how an investigation worked, even if the thought of her crew being temporary suspects made her squirrelly. She let his comment slide and surveyed him from head to toe. "You weren't hurt?"

"No. Whoever was firing seemed to be aiming at the buildings, not at any of us. Based on several things, Blankenship and I think this was more scare tactic than attempted murder."

The unspoken words hung in the air. *If he'd wanted us dead, then we'd be dead.*

Who was to say that whoever was targeting her wouldn't shift from fear to murder in order to get what he wanted?

And who even knew what he wanted?

"You don't need to come back from your vacation, Jacob." Angie pressed the phone tighter against her ear and walked to her bedroom window on the second floor of the main house. From this vantage point, she could see across the land behind the barn to the canyon in the distance. The summer sun wouldn't set for a few hours, but dark cumulonimbus clouds built in the western sky, lightning chasing between them as they rushed closer.

It was normally a sight she loved, but today it couldn't keep her from staring toward the ranch. Multiple law-enforcement vehicles had passed on the road in front of the house in the past few minutes, indicating they were probably done collecting evidence. It had been hours since Lincoln had banished her to the house with a female deputy.

One who'd stared at Linc with the kind of adoring big brown eyes usually reserved for TV romance movies.

Linc hadn't seemed to notice.

That shouldn't have given her a sense of triumph.

The deputy was downstairs now, keeping an eye on her from a distance. For most of the afternoon, the younger woman had tried to distract Angie with conversation, but not much had worked. When Jacob had called, Angie had fled to her room, craving some time to herself. She was jealous of Rosa, who was alone in her office finding off-site lodging for the researchers.

Once she got her brother off the line, Angie might get some alone time as well. For now, he was saying his piece. "Ang, this is too big for you to handle alone."

"I'm not alone. Half of the sheriff's department is here. Rosa, Danny and Wiley are at the ranch." She squinted as a man walked around the corner of the house, headed toward the small barn at the rear of the property. His familiar gait would be recognizable anywhere, although there was a hitch in his step she hadn't noticed before. "And Linc has arrived."

Where was he going? He had his phone to his ear, and he disappeared around the side of the barn, likely looking for somewhere private for his phone call.

To whom?

Angie let the curtain fall. It wasn't her business, but wondering about his actions kept her from thinking about worse things.

This land had always been her safe place. But now? She shuddered.

From a hotel room in London, her brother exhaled heavily. It was late in the evening there, and he and his little family ought to be settling in to rest after tea or some other very British activity. Instead, he was talking to her, the brother in him unable to stop worrying while the investigator in him couldn't stop asking questions.

The selfish part of her wanted him to chuck his vacation and come home.

But the sister in her couldn't let him sacrifice a trip he and Ivy had been dreaming about. "I'm fine."

"Look, you stepped up to the plate a couple of years ago when Ivy was in trouble. You were there when I was hurt. I can't—"

"Jacob, I have no proof this is about me. When Ivy was in trouble, someone was actively hunting her. When you were hurt, it was my job to help you get better." She dug her teeth into her lower lip. It had been her job, but with Linc's help.

She cleared her throat. "I'm guessing someone had a beef with Ellis, though I can't imagine what." Ellis West had worked at the ranch for a little over six months, and he'd spent most of his time with the cattle. While his father had worked at the ranch years ago, before he died in a car accident, she didn't know Ellis well. His job fell under Rosa's supervision, not hers.

"Someone came at you last night, Ang."

"You think I forgot?" The terror would live in her memory forever, although she was trying to squash it. "Maybe they thought I saw something. But he tipped his hand today with that sniper act. Now law enforcement is on high alert. Trying again would be foolish."

That's what she told herself, anyway. But as the day raced toward night and the law-enforcement officers left the property, she was growing less confident.

"I'd feel better if you went somewhere else for tonight, at least."

"I'll be fine." *Hopefully.* "Besides, I hear the protestors are at the gate again. That ought to scare potential bad guys away."

"Not funny, especially since they're probably involved."

"The deputies spoke to them today, and they're checking alibis. You taught me how to defend myself. There's nothing to worry about." *I hope.*

Besides, she didn't want company. She wanted time to process. The events of the past twenty-four hours threatened to swamp her if she didn't find a journal and write them out in bullet points, praying over each one. She needed time with God that didn't involve scattered, angry prayers like the ones she'd spouted as she navigated the roads from Vegas. She didn't need the threat of someone walking in on her outpouring of emotion.

A series of attacks. A dying dream. A burning humiliation.

While some issues were bigger than others, all of them blended into a toxic stew that needed to be filtered.

"I'll set the alarm. I'll call for help if I need to. You enjoy your week and keep my niece safe. If something is going on, then we want Wren as far away as possible." That precious little girl had been through enough.

Across the ocean, Jacob muttered something that sounded like resignation.

Angie almost smiled. Appealing to his feelings for his wife and daughter was a sure way to sway him.

She refused to let that make her jealous. Her brother had something she'd never been able to find. Something she'd never be able to trust in, even if she did manage to locate it in this mess of a world.

"Fine." Jacob clipped out the word, probably to make sure she knew he wasn't happy. "But if anything else happens, I want to know."

"Fine."

"Also, I want Linc to stay tonight."

"Absolutely not." Linc had been on the property all day, and she'd been keenly aware of every move he'd made. She didn't need the distraction.

"It's the only way I'm staying in Europe."

He had her backed into a corner. "Fine." She ground out the word. She'd do anything to make her family happy, including, she supposed, allowing Lincoln Tucker to sleep in the storage room connected to the barn.

He certainly wasn't staying in her house.

After goodbyes and a promise to give Wren a hug, Jacob disconnected the call.

The deputy's voice floated from downstairs. "Ms. Garcia?"

Pocketing her phone, Angie went to the door, unwilling to head down for more empty conversation, no matter how well-meaning the young deputy was. "I'm here."

"I'm heading out. Agent Tucker is on his way in as soon as he finishes taking a phone call. Do you need anything?"

Angie sagged against the doorframe. Maybe she'd be able to find five minutes of quiet. "I'm good. Be safe."

"You, too." The downstairs floor creaked slightly, then the alarm chimed to indicate a door had been opened. At the front of the house, a car started.

Exhaling slowly, Angie walked to the window. If she could get even two minutes to herself, it would be something. She pulled back the corner of the curtain.

Linc was nowhere to be seen. She'd have heard him come into the house because the door chime on the alarm would have indicated he'd opened the door. With a storm coming in fast, he should get inside.

Movement at the fence along a ravine beyond the barn kept her from dropping the curtain into place. Surely Linc wasn't all the way out there.

Angie squinted into the fading light as dark clouds drew closer. Was that…?

A horse. The animal was saddled and facing the fence, shaking his head as though he was caught on something. As the brown horse tossed his head, he turned slightly, revealing a large white patch along his hindquarters.

Chance.

Ellis West's horse.

The animal hadn't been there ten minutes earlier. Where had he come from?

She bolted down the stairs and out the front door, hoping to catch the deputy before she left, but a puff of orange dirt along the driveway indicated it was too late.

In the distance, thunder rumbled, rolling from the canyon.

She couldn't leave the horse in the brewing storm. Judging by the height of the cloud tops, it promised to be a raging one.

Linc was somewhere around the barn, and the fence where Chance was caught was a few hundred yards beyond. He'd be able to hear her, maybe even see her if she ran into any trouble.

Another roll of thunder, followed by a gust that rattled the windows, made up her mind. Linc might have told her to stay inside, but she couldn't leave a helpless animal in a storm.

She raced across the downstairs, then passed through the mudroom, snagging her raincoat on the way, and headed out the side door.

The world had changed in the moments she'd been making her decision. Dark clouds roiled overhead. The scent of rain and dust blew on the stiff breeze that whipped across the open land from the direction of the canyon. Lightning crisscrossed the sky, too close for comfort. She was definitely within the ten-mile strike zone. She needed to move quickly.

Running past the barn, she called for Linc, but her voice was carried away by the wind.

Surely he'd know where she went. If she could see Chance from the house, Linc should be able to see him from the barn.

As she neared the horse, he stopped moving and watched her with wide eyes. She'd helped train him when he came to the ranch a few years earlier, so he knew her. Hopefully that would be enough to calm him.

Angie held her hands out toward the massive creature, eyeing him from nose to tail. He didn't appear to be injured, but his reins were tangled in the top fence rail, pinning him close to the rough wood. "It's okay, buddy. I'm going to get you into the barn, where it's safe."

She stepped closer, and Chance eyed her warily. He tried to move away, but he was tethered too tightly to the fence.

She halted her forward progress, not wanting to spook him into hurting himself. "You know me, buddy. It's okay."

As the wind gusted again, she studied the reins and eased closer to the fence, facing the horse with her back to the trees.

Something about those reins didn't look right.

Angie leaned closer. They weren't snagged. They were looped around and knotted.

She jumped, and Chance jerked his head, whinnying loudly.

This wasn't an accident. Chance hadn't gotten caught in the fence. He'd been tied there by someone who'd known she wouldn't be able to resist rescuing the animal.

Heart rising into her throat, Angie turned as the rain unleashed. "Linc!" she yelled toward the barn, hoping he'd hear and praying she was wrong.

But she was right.

A shadowy figure leaped from the woods and grabbed her by the arm. A gloved hand covered her mouth as the man pulled her against his chest and lifted her feet from the ground, hefting her into the trees where a gray truck waited with the doors open, ready to steal her.

Forever.

FIVE

Tucking his phone into his pocket, Linc stared at the angry sky as a wind gust nearly shoved him backward. The next available MRI appointment wasn't for two weeks.

Two weeks until he'd know the extent of his injuries and whether he could return to full duty, be the man he was supposed to be.

Lord...please. Pleading made him feel weak, as though he was taking from God instead of offering anything of value.

He'd never felt more worthless.

The sky unleashed a furious deluge. He ducked around the corner under the lean-to at the rear of the barn, where the Garcias kept their father's old farm trucks. He needed to get to the house, to make sure—

"Linc!" The wind screamed his name.

Or was that Angie?

She couldn't have left the house. He'd have seen her.

Except he'd been walking along the side of the barn with the house out of sight.

Linc and the sheriff had been clear she was safer inside, but Angie was headstrong.

Ignoring the rain, Linc walked to the edge of the overhang. Maybe he was hearing things.

Lightning struck on the far side of the ravine, beyond the fence. Thunder crashed.

A horse's frantic squeal followed.

Linc squinted against the storm.

There. Against the fence, a horse pulled at his reins, which were tangled in the rails. Had Angie come outside to—

Movement to the left jerked his attention from the animal.

A man, dressed in dark clothing with a hood over his head, was dragging Angie into the trees. She kicked, but her fight was useless.

Linc bolted forward, his hand on his weapon. The quick motion shot pain down his spine. Adrenaline rattled through him. "Federal agent! Let her go!"

Raging wind threw the words against the barn.

The man hesitated.

It was a nightmarish repeat of the previous night.

The rain fell harder, whipping between them as Linc edged closer and the man tried to drag Angie farther. His movements were slowed by her struggling.

Why didn't he let her go? There was no way he could escape with Angie hindering his speed and maneuverability.

Linc maintained his steady approach, moving as quickly as he dared with his vision hampered by the rain. Maybe the man had an accomplice waiting in the woods, or he planned to kill Angie rather than kidnap her.

The thought chilled him more than the slashing rain. "Let her go!" The last thing he wanted was a physical altercation, the very thing he'd been warned by the doctors to avoid, but hesitation could sign Angie's death warrant.

The man pulled Angie tighter against him with one hand as he reached behind his back with the other.

It was likely he had a weapon tucked in his waistband.

Time had run out.

As Linc rushed forward, Angie seemed to grasp what was happening. She went limp, then straightened, driving her elbows into her assailant's ribs.

It was an awkward blow, but it was enough to cause the man to stumble.

Linc dove into the fray, and the three of them tumbled to the ground in a heap.

Angie gasped.

The man cursed.

Linc landed hard, one shoulder driving into the man's chest and the other colliding with Angie's shoulder. White heat shot dancing lights and dark spots into his vision.

Had they been struck by lightning?

No. This bolt was from inside. It turned his muscles and mind to mush.

Angie's assailant shoved Lincoln to the side, then scrambled to his feet.

Linc tried to stand, but he got to one knee before a wave of dizziness pinned him to the ground. If the guy doubled back and dealt another blow, there would be nothing Linc could do to stop him.

But the dark figure ran into the trees. Over the pounding rain, an engine roared, then he could hear a vehicle race away.

Dropping his chin to his chest, Lincoln gulped air and waited for the pain to subside. *Please, Lord.* It had to stop. This couldn't be the fatal blow.

The world wobbled. Black haze crowded in as his ears rang. He was helpless. Useless.

Angie dropped to her knees and rested a hand on his shoulder. "Linc, look at me." Gently, she tilted his chin, the simple gesture ripping pain down his spine.

He struggled to bring the world into focus as rain ran down his face.

Her green eyes locked on to his, wide with terror. "We have to go."

He could do this. He *had* to do this.

And he'd do it without her lifting him like a flopping rag

doll. It took all of his strength to rise. "I need to call this in." The horizon was rocking back and forth, but he stayed on his feet.

"The horse." Angie stood with him, keeping one hand on his arm as she stretched the other toward the animal, who jerked at his reins. "I can't leave Chance."

She'd never let an animal suffer in this weather, and neither would he. Linc drew his pistol and faced the woods, wrestling the pain. "Get the horse."

Before he knew it, she was leading the animal toward him. Quickly, with Linc watching the woods and Angie leading the skittish horse, they made their way toward the barn.

Each step caused a jolt of fresh pain. He took them one at a time, fighting to keep the darkness at bay. If these were the last steps he ever took…

He shoved aside the thought. Getting Angie to safety was vital. He had no choice but to soldier on.

Linc shut the barn doors against the deluge, grateful for the rollers that made the massive door slide easily along the concrete floor. The pain between his shoulders felt like a creature was gnawing on his spinal cord, but the more he moved, the less he felt like he was falling into an abyss. His vision came into focus as the pain receded.

As Angie led Chance into a stall, Linc glanced around the barn. Three stalls lined each side of the wide center aisle, where the family's horses, Flynn and Shiloh, typically sheltered. The wood ceiling was high, providing for storage above. At the far end of the space, a closed door separated the office and storage from the rest of the building.

The smell of horses and hay hovered in the air. There was something comforting about the familiar scents that made him feel almost normal.

Rain pounded the metal roof and lashed the sides of the

barn, making it difficult to hear anything outside. There were no windows. They were boxed in.

He didn't like it.

Angie was talking quietly to the skittish horse as she removed his tack.

Gently pulling his head to one side, hoping to stretch away the pain, Linc took out his phone.

No service.

Cell signal was weak on a normal day. During a storm like this one, they didn't have a chance. He was on his own.

He pocketed the device and walked slowly to the stall to keep from spooking Chance, who had finally calmed. He studied the animal as Angie brushed him. "I don't recognize this guy."

"He's Ellis's horse." She slowly moved around the animal, scratching his nose before she took a position on his opposite side, facing Linc.

Why was Ellis's saddled horse roaming Fairweather? They'd seen no sign of Ellis all day.

Thunder cracked nearby, and Chance jumped.

Angie shushed him, humming a wordless song as she brushed his coat.

It was tough to tell if Angie was soothing the horse or herself. "How are you doing?"

"I'd rather not talk about it while I'm dealing with a skittish horse."

As though he understood, Chance jerked his head like he was about to buck.

With a pointed look at Linc, Angie steadied the horse. "I'll deal with my feelings later."

There she went, focusing on the task and not on what was happening inside of her. It was her worst habit.

"I'd rather talk about you." She let her eyes follow the path of the brush as she worked. "What happened out there?"

Linc's shoulders stiffened, zinging pain through him. He schooled his expression.

When the horse tensed, Linc stepped away from the stall and shoved his hands into his pockets. "Got the wind knocked out of me."

"Hmm." Angie's gaze flicked to him, then to Chance. "You move like a robot, and you're completely pale. What's the deal?" Rounding the horse, she scratched Chance's nose, then grabbed a bucket and eased out of the stall, closing the door behind her. She stopped in front of Lincoln. "How bad are you hurt?"

The fact that he'd foundered enough for her to notice was humiliating. If he'd lost consciousness or had been unable to get off the ground, she could have died.

He'd failed her. So, no, he didn't want to discuss it.

"Linc…" She walked over to a faucet a few feet from the floor and filled the bucket. The rush of water drowned out every other sound.

He watched, feeling helpless. Even the weight of a five-gallon bucket was too much for him at the moment.

Angie didn't speak until she'd settled the bucket in front of Chance and stepped into the aisle, latching the stall behind her. She faced Lincoln. "Tell the truth, then I'll tell you how I'm really feeling."

Lincoln leaned against a stall door and crossed his arms over his chest. It was a rare offer, and it might be the only way to get her to speak truthfully.

Was he willing to make the sacrifice?

Across the aisle, Angie mimicked his posture, her gaze holding a challenge.

Rain lashed the roof harder, filling the space with noise. The roar outside and the silence inside made him feel as though he'd stepped outside of time, as though anything that happened in the barn could be left there when the storm ended.

With a loud exhale, he made his decision. "A few weeks ago, we were practicing a rappelling drill. I was about twelve feet up when…" He pursed his lips, not quite ready to admit he'd gotten cocky. Maybe he'd been showing off. Maybe he'd been careless. "Long story short, I landed flat on my back, staring at the sky."

"Linc." Angie's hands thumped against the stall door.

Chance looked up, then went back to drinking water.

Angie winced. "How bad?" A shadow crossed her features. Likely his story brought memories of Jacob's pain.

He might as well tell all, or she'd invent an injury far worse than the one he suffered. "I ruptured a disc in my cervical spine. The MRI showed it putting pressure on my spinal cord. Made my arms numb. Brought on some epic headaches." The pounding pain that pulsed in his eyeballs had been the worst. He'd refused stronger painkillers, having seen in the military how quickly opioid addiction could take hold.

"That's why you're available here instead of being active on the team."

Pain arced up Linc's neck as he nodded. Available? More like useless.

Except… There was no way anyone could watch Angie 24/7. Resources were stretched too thin. If he wasn't injured, she'd probably be here without protection.

For a few minutes, the only sound was the squall outside and Chance's huffing as he made himself comfortable.

Right when he thought the conversation was over, Angie broke the silence. "What's your prognosis?"

That was the part he had never spoken aloud, barely acknowledging it when Dr. Collins had studied her tablet for an eternity before handing over her thoughts.

But here, in this isolated moment, the pressure squeezed his chest until words found their way out. "Surgery is risky.

Could leave me paralyzed from the neck down. I can do physical therapy, but the doc thinks…"

He closed his eyes. The doc thought the worst.

That he'd lost his job and himself…forever.

Linc was quiet so long, Angie wondered if he would ever speak again.

His expression was nearly the same as when Jacob had first been moved from Brooke Army Medical Center in Houston to the VA center in Las Vegas. That had been the first time Linc had been able to visit her brother and to see the extent of his injuries. They'd been unsure if he'd recover enough to lead a normal life, let alone serve his country again.

She'd found Linc in a small waiting room at the end of the hall, staring out a window, struggling to hold himself together. Jacob's injuries had been extensive after an IED blast in Afghanistan, and his rehabilitation had been grueling. Linc had never wanted her brother to see the effect the initial sight of Jacob's pain had inflicted on him.

That day, he'd become more than Jacob's battle buddy and best friend, at least to her. Without even considering whether he'd want her to or not, she'd rested her hand on his back and her head on his shoulder. She'd understood his pain. Had felt the way they shared the struggle in a way that bonded them immediately.

When he'd pulled her free hand to his chest and held on tight, they'd simply stood with one another and grieved what had happened and sought strength for what was to come. They had solidified a friendship, a partnership forged in working together to make sure Jacob got well as they shielded her mother from the worst of his pain.

Angie had kept on a brave, smiling face at the hospital, at the rehab center and at the house…

Until the night she hadn't.

Now she'd gone too far, asking personal questions when everything between them had begun to settle into cordiality.

She needed a distraction. Needed to not think about the pain in her ribs where that man's arm had dug so deep she likely had a bruise. Needed to not think about what would have happened if Linc hadn't rescued her.

Again.

Right now, she could be…

A shudder ran through her. She could be anywhere. The victim of anything.

Chance snorted, probably sensing her unease.

She forced even breaths to keep from riling the horse and so Lincoln wouldn't recognize her fear.

Leaning on him was not an option. Not after what had happened the last time.

There was also no way she could close the space between them to hug him or extend comfort.

Because the last time she'd reached out to him that way, she'd kissed him. She'd kissed him and then pushed for more in an effort to cover her roiling, out-of-control grief and fear.

Although she wasn't that person any longer, Linc would likely rebuff any touch she offered.

So she stood as the rain pelted the roof and the wind rattled the doors and Chance slurped water from his bucket.

Stood…and waited for whatever came next.

With a huff, Linc spoke. "The chances of me returning to what I love are slim. Likely, once we're all the way through this, I can live what most people would call a normal life. Drive, eat, sleep, work a job somewhere…all without fear and with minimal pain." He finally faced her, but his gaze landed at her feet. "Climbing? Strenuous hiking? Wrestling with the occasional bad guy? Anything that relates to the job I love?" His hand sliced the air. "Out of the question."

At his declaration, even the storm outside seemed to still.

The rain pounded the roof with less ferocity, and the wind eased. It was as though the whole world heard the weight of grief in Linc's voice and had responded in kind.

"I'm sorry." What else could she say? How did someone comfort a man who'd been told he might lose everything he held dear?

Linc's life was his job. He'd said so the night he told her he respected her too much to use her. He'd tacked on a speech about how he didn't want a relationship. Never planned to get married. All he wanted to do was exactly what he was doing with the National Park Service.

Every word had made her feel smaller. More rejected. Until it became not about the physical line she'd tried to cross, but about her personally. Never good enough. Never worthy of love. Never worthy of a man who stayed.

Even now, all these years later, her cheeks and neck burned at the memory of her behavior and of his rejection.

No way would she let him see her discomfort. She turned, opened the stall and grabbed the half-full bucket Chance had been drinking from. She crossed to the faucet, then refilled it and set it into place before she felt as though she could speak in a normal voice.

"You know… They told Jacob he'd never be the same again. That he'd be in pain the rest of his life. And now he's out working with you, doing all of the things the experts told him he'd never be able to do." The external forces from the blast in Afghanistan had scrambled her brother's insides and left him in intense pain. His recovery had been grueling, but he'd overcome. He'd—

"Don't act like his life is all sunshine. He can do everything except the one thing he wanted most." Linc's words were bitter.

Angie dug her teeth into her lower lip. Linc was right, to an extent. Her brother's internal injuries had ensured he would never have another child of his own.

Through a twist no one saw coming, he'd learned a couple of years after the IED explosion that he'd previously fathered a child with his ex-fiancée, who was now his wife. Wren was a joy to the entire family.

Still, Jacob would never have another.

"Some things can't be fixed. Some things can. And do you know what? I plan to be one of the ones who beats this." Linc knocked twice on the stall behind him and straightened. "It sounds like the rain is letting up. Will Chance be okay out here by himself?" He glanced at his phone, made a face, then pocketed it again. "I don't have service yet. You?"

Well, sharing time was over. Angie hesitated. There was so much more to say. He'd spilled his pain onto the concrete and she'd left it there, unable to help him. It felt wrong. There must be something she could do. A Linc who couldn't roam the canyon freely in service to others simply wasn't Linc.

"Angie? Cell service?" He said the words in a clipped tone, impatience rising.

Probably because he believed he'd said too much. Rather than argue, she pulled the phone from her jacket pocket. "No bars. Sorry. The rain's going to have to ease more before you get any bars. That's why I have a landline. Sometimes out here, cell signal is worthless."

"I don't like that, especially now." He glanced at his phone again. "I'm glad you have a landline, but if you're out on the ranch like you were today, how are you going to communicate when the weather wrecks your signal?" His chin rose and he pinned her gaze. "You're no longer dealing with a skittish horse, so I'm going to ask again. Are you okay? You said if I talked, you'd talk. So talk."

She'd known the conversation would eventually return to her. She'd kind of hoped he'd forgotten her promise. As much as she'd rather pretend nothing had happened, she'd have to hand him something or he'd hound her until she cracked.

There would be no more cracking in front of Lincoln Tucker.

Besides, she had Jesus now. He could get her through anything.

"I'm a little bit sore, but—"

"Sore?" Lincoln crossed the wide aisle in two long steps and stopped in front of her. His blue eyes were dark. "How so? Did he hurt you?" His hand hovered between them as though he planned to touch her.

Angie stepped aside. "I'm not hurt. He had on a watch or something. It pressed into my ribs. I'm certain nothing is broken. At the worst, I'll have a bruise." *And a few nightmares.*

No need to pass that along. She could deal with it herself. Linc didn't need a shivering victim on his plate, not with all he was already dealing with.

Thunder rolled across the space, a distant wave that indicated the storm had passed over them and was moving on. The rain on the roof had slackened to a gentle shower. "I think the weather's about spent itself, and Chance is calm enough for some hay. I'll feed him, then we can get to the house and you can use the landline to call out." She backed another step away from him, toward the door to the storage area and the stairs to the haymow. "I'll have to toss a bale down from upstairs. Later I'll call Rosa to let her know Chance is here." She was babbling. Too many random words were pouring out, but she couldn't stop them.

It was nerves. Or Linc. Or fear. Or a thousand other things she never wanted to admit lived inside of her.

Linc matched her step for step as she backed toward the door. "You stay down here. I'll go up. I'd rather clear the building before I let you go anywhere by yourself."

Her foot dragged on the concrete and she stumbled to a stop. Her eyes went to the haymow above them. "You think someone's up there?"

"I think someone is everywhere. Especially now."

That statement was way too ominous for her taste. It sounded too much like paranoia. Fear. Things that held her back. Turning, she strode for the door. "Nobody is up there. If they were, they'd have already made themselves known."

She was nearly to the door when Linc's strong arms grabbed her from behind and dragged her against the wall of his chest. "Angie, stop."

A flash of terror raced through her at the memory of arms that intended to harm her. Of a faceless figure dragging her into the woods.

If Linc hadn't arrived when he—

"Angie, listen." Gently, he pulled her away from the door. "Don't touch anything. I'm going to let you go, but don't touch anything."

"What are you—" She scanned the area. What had he seen? A gun? A bomb? Some sort of device that—

Her eyes caught on the door and she froze. Near the handle, smeared fingerprints marred the metal. Something that looked like dark paint had dripped on the pristine concrete floor.

Her heart pounded harder. Those fingerprints… Those drops… They weren't paint.

They were blood.

SIX

"Back away, Angie. Now." With one hand, Linc turned Angie around and aimed her toward the opposite end of the barn. He reached for his phone with the other, praying the rain had eased enough to give him a signal. One bar showed on the screen. It had better be enough. Detective Blankenship needed to get to the barn immediately. So did his team's crime-scene unit.

He had a horrible feeling that Ellis West's whereabouts weren't going to be a mystery for much longer.

"Linc…" Angie hesitated, her voice shaking as she said his name.

She hadn't asked him for help since…

Well, since Jacob had been injured and they'd been caring for him together. Before her grief drove her into his arms and he'd had to tell her no, not only because he couldn't exploit her vulnerability, but also because he couldn't be the kind of man she deserved to have in her life.

For the first time, he saw open fear in her expression. She was struggling to bury it, and she was failing. He needed to stop being an investigator for half a second. Take a deep breath. Focus on her.

As soon as he called the detective.

His heart breaking for Angie, wrestling the line between duty and compassion, he guided her toward the barn door, then pulled her close, wrapping his arm around her waist and holding her against his side. He thumbed his phone with his free hand until he found Blankenship's number.

When she answered, he kept it brief. "It's Tucker. Bring the team to the horse barn behind the main house. I think I know where West is. And…" How to say this without upsetting Angie? "Bring Ortiz." Blankenship would know the name. The coroner would need to be on-site, he had no doubt.

As soon as she'd confirmed, Linc killed the call, pocketed his phone and turned so Angie's back was to the door. He held her to his chest and simply let her rest there, her face pressed against his shoulder. It wasn't advisable for him to have her in his arms, but he also wasn't going to send her away to battle her fears and grief alone.

She shook, her breathing ragged. "What's happening?"

Linc stared over her head at the door, which still looked new after the rebuild of the barn following an arsonist's attempt to destroy it a couple of years prior. The metal door was pristine except for the smears of blood around the handle. Too much blood to have come from a mere cut. Had he walked to the door sooner, he'd have seen the evidence long before Angie had come close to touching it.

"Linc? Answer me." Angie tried to pull away, but he tightened his grip. She didn't need to see any more than she already had. There were enough horrible imagined images already swirling in her brain, he was sure. There was no need to cement them with reality.

In the aftermath of the wind and rain, the barn was eerily quiet, adding to the surreal feeling of the moment. Linc wished he could make all of the horror go away. "I don't know exactly what's going on, but you need to trust me. As much as you think you want to know the details, believe me, you don't." Too many nightmarish scenes lived in his head. Too many murders. Too many fallen hikers. Too many victims. Every one of them resided in his memory. Every one of them awoke him at night, sometimes in a cold sweat that wouldn't let him fall into the peaceful darkness of sleep.

He'd spare Angie that, at least. Sometimes, imagination was worse than reality. Other times, it wasn't. Because if his suspicions were right, Ellis West was about to join that never-ending line of horrifying images that he could never forget.

He needed to get her into the house, but he also needed to keep his eye on her and on what he now recognized as a crime scene. They should have checked the barn earlier in the day, but the detectives had been focused on the scene of her assault and the site at the ranch, assuming the two scenes were connected.

Well, they'd officially passed making assumptions. It was now almost a certainty that Ellis's disappearance and Angie's confrontation were part of the same heinous crime.

He had no idea how long they stood silently with her warm against his chest before Angie's phone chimed. She eased away from him and pressed the screen. "It's the deputies. They're at the gate. I let them in."

Within moments, several cars approached from the direction of the main gate. His time to comfort Angie was over. Now he needed to shift into work mode. Gently, he eased her away from him. "I need you to go to the house, okay?" He spoke to her in much the same way Angie had spoken to the skittish Chance earlier. With their history and the tension of her situation, she could easily buck.

He guided her to the entrance as he spoke, then tugged the door open, working hard to ignore the fresh pain in his back.

A female deputy entered the corral and walked closer. She gave Lincoln a terse nod as she rested a hand on Angie's back. "Hey, Ang. Let's go inside while these guys work."

When Angie saw the woman, her face registered recognition and she seemed to relax slightly. She pulled away from

Lincoln, following the auburn-haired deputy without a word and, thankfully, without looking back.

She'd be in good hands.

He watched her walk away until Detective Blankenship approached with her department's crime-scene investigators, who were already gearing up and heading into the barn.

They were pulling out all of the stops on this one. *Good.*

Blankenship hung back with him in the corral as the crew entered the barn and immediately started taking photos. "What are you thinking?"

He shot her a look. No need to answer. There was no doubt that their suspicions matched perfectly.

She sighed. "I was hoping for a different outcome." Looking over her shoulder toward the house, she frowned. "You think our bad guy believes Angie saw something last night when she arrived home?"

"Most likely. It would explain the attacks last night and this afternoon, as well as the shooting at the cabins. When she pulled up, they could have been here in the barn. She might have spooked them into thinking they had a witness on their hands. They could have decided…" No need to finish that sentence. He didn't need that kind of potential horror living rent-free with the other terrible images in his head.

One of the techs appeared in the doorway and waved them over.

Blankenship passed him a set of gloves. "Ready for a new nightmare?"

He took the gloves, although he had his own, but didn't respond.

Blankenship led the way through the barn that had been a refuge moments earlier.

From his stall, Chance watched the proceedings with interest, though he seemed calm.

If only Linc felt that kind of peace.

At the door, he and Blankenship both stopped, scanning the scene inside. A wide hallway led straight through to the back of the barn. To the left, the office door was open. To the right, the door that led to a storage space and the stairs to the loft was closed.

In the center of the aisle, a man was pitched forward in a wooden chair. His hands were tied behind him, and his ankles were bound to the chair's legs. He wasn't wearing a shirt, and blood pooled beneath him on the concrete. The way his body slumped, it was clear he was past saving.

Training kept Linc from backing away. From the amount of blood and the marks on his face, arms and bare chest, the man had been beaten until his body succumbed to the brutality.

Linc swallowed the revulsion that rose at the evidence of such brutal cruelty. It never seemed to dim, no matter how long he was on the job.

He cleared his throat. "This is Ellis West?"

It took a moment for Blankenship to answer. "His face is so swollen I can't make a totally positive identification but that would be my assumption." She walked a wide berth around the man and studied his back. "It's him. West had a distinct tribal tattoo down his spine. It's damaged but still visible."

Linc searched for footprints, but there was nothing but blood and clumps of mud on the concrete, likely from the killer's boots. There was nothing to identify the attacker, but the crime-scene unit would dust for prints and gather evidence. "We don't have much to go on."

"No, but we do have Ellis. I doubt our killer planned to leave him here like this. Chances are high he was forced to flee when Angie came home, and then, with our presence on the property, he wasn't able to return and clean his mess."

Linc pursed his lips and turned away from the body. He walked to the door and stared into the outside world, where the sun was beginning to set. "Why basically torture the guy?

What did someone want from him?" It was possible this wasn't about Angie at all. Someone had a clear beef with Ellis, and they'd taken their time causing him pain. Whatever it was about, it was either deeply personal, or it was the work of an incredibly depraved mind.

"We'll take a deeper dive into his background, but off the top, I have no idea. I looked at his file at the ranch. They ran thorough background checks before they hired him, and he came out with a spotless record outside of a couple of speeding tickets when he was a teenager. That's not to say everything is spotless in his world, though. He could have been running with the wrong people and never got caught. Could have seen something somebody didn't want him to see. Could have crossed the wrong person."

"What about his family?" There could be a vendetta there.

"Mom is a nurse at a local clinic. Dad was killed in a car accident about ten years ago. Sister is married to a warehouse manager and stays at home with two kids."

Nothing raised alarm bells there. "Why bring Ellis here if this started at his cabin? Rosa was with her mother. The other two hands were away. The researchers are out in the canyon. No one was there. Somebody injured the guy in his quarters, loaded him into a vehicle and brought him here. Then they either hid his horse or stumbled upon the animal and brought him here to bait Angie. That's a lot of chances to be seen and a lot of evidence to risk leaving behind."

"Maybe the killer didn't realize everyone else was gone? Whoever brought West here may have known Angie was in Vegas and assumed they wouldn't be interrupted. Probably thought they'd have time to do whatever they'd planned, then clean up behind themselves."

"But Angie came home early."

"And they wound up with a bigger problem."

Linc walked up the barn's aisle to the door and looked at the house.

From the dining-room window, Angie was watching the barn.

He turned to the detective. "If they knew her movements, then it's possible it's someone close to her. Someone who has access. Angie is still in danger."

"You cannot tell Jacob about this." Angie shook her hands by her sides as she walked across the living room. So much nervous energy and terror coursed through her that she was tempted to do something she never did.

She was six seconds from strapping on running shoes. If only she could push herself until she dropped and not think of anything else. Until all of this energy poured out of her in sweat and tears. Forget that it was past midnight and the crime-scene unit had just left her property. Again. That someone had been murdered mere feet from her home. That someone had tried to kill her three times. All she wanted was to escape. Maybe if she ran far enough, she'd wake up and this would all be a terrible nightmare.

She stopped in front of the couch and turned toward the kitchen.

It had to be a dream, because Lincoln Tucker was in her home in the dark of night, and that hadn't happened since Jacob's recovery.

There was another vision she didn't need.

Linc stood in the middle of the kitchen, watching her pace. He was so calm she wanted to scream to see if he could be rattled.

How could he be so undisturbed? They'd found a murdered man in her barn. A man who worked for her. This was escalating so fast her head was spinning from the altitude change.

She ripped a hair band from her wrist and pulled her hair into a ponytail, seeking any sort of normal constructive behavior, no matter how minor. "Linc, seriously. You can't tell Jacob."

"He's going to find out."

"He'll come home, and I can't let him. You're here. You're handling it. Right?"

"I'm trying my best." There was something bitter in his tone.

Frowning, Angie sank onto the edge of the oversize chair by the huge stone fireplace. *Right.* Linc was injured. He might even be worse after defending her this afternoon.

Yet here she was worried about her brother's vacation.

This was not her rational self. This was her emotional self. Stomping around the living room. Making demands. Feeling as though her skeleton might crawl out of her skin. She hadn't been this out of control since—

Since the night everything had fallen apart. When the dam holding her fear and anger and pain over her brother's injury had burst under the weight of exhaustion. That night, she'd ranted and raged like this…and the outlet she'd sought had been Lincoln's arms. That night, she'd asked him for everything, and he'd politely extricated himself from her embrace, packed his things in the guest room and left.

The long nights sitting at the kitchen table together had ended. The friendship that had morphed into something more through the trial of Jacob's recovery had died.

He'd simply…vanished. Afterward, Linc helped when he could, but his full-time presence was gone.

She'd resented him at first. Had wanted to hate him. But after she'd come to her senses and later handed over her life to Jesus, she'd realized what she'd asked of the man. How much she'd demanded they both compromise.

All of her frustration and anger had morphed into a burning humiliation over her own actions, one that made her uncomfortable around the man she'd once opened her heart to.

The one who'd rejected her. After all, he could have told her no and stepped away. But no. He'd packed and left. She hadn't been worth staying for.

It was a different kind of leaving than what Owen had done to her, but it was leaving nonetheless. She'd been too much to handle. She'd been too needy and emotional. She'd let him see a vulnerability she hadn't shown to anyone since Owen's betrayal.

Well, that mistake wouldn't happen again.

This was why she focused on what she could do. This was why she made sure there was a job in front of her at all times. Like a shark, if she kept moving from one task to the next, she wouldn't drown.

"Okay." Angie stood and balled her fists, refusing to fidget any longer. It made her look overly emotional and weak. "What do we do now?" She needed a goal. Something to focus on.

Linc didn't leave his spot in the center of the kitchen, but he rested his hands on the island. "Now? You sleep. You have to get some rest. How long has it been?"

She'd fallen asleep sitting on the couch in the dark hours of the previous morning, when the sheriff had been gathering evidence on the porch. It probably hadn't been enough.

But the thought of going upstairs to her room and closing her eyes terrified her more than she wanted to admit. If she turned out the lights and tried to lie still, she might not be able to get the day out of her head. Her brain would construct pictures of the scene in the barn, the one Lincoln hadn't let her see. She'd think too much about the gunshots and mayhem and death in her own backyard, and she might lose herself completely.

Besides, Linc had no room to talk. "You've had less sleep than me." She planted her feet, not willing to step closer to him but needing to stand her ground. Leaning forward slightly, she crossed her arms and studied his face. Dark circles under his blue eyes spoke of his fatigue. Lines furrowing his forehead told the story of his pain. "You don't look so good."

He puffed his cheeks and blew out a slow breath, almost as though he was leaking out frustration that threatened to explode without a pressure release.

Good. Maybe she needed to get under his skin.

"Angie, I know what this is about." He leveled his gaze at her and seemed to stare straight into her brain.

There was no doubt what he was referring to.

She felt her nostrils flare, but she wasn't sure if the response was anger or shock. Surely he wasn't going to bring up their past. Not now. Not with the coroner still en route from her ranch to the medical examiner's office. Not with crime-scene tape around her barn. Not with fresh bruises on her body and soul.

Linc took a deep breath and stared at the beams in the ceiling. "I'm sorry."

The soft words slammed into her chest and rocked her off her feet. It wasn't at all what she'd expected. She sat hard in the chair. "Sorry?" She hadn't wanted to engage in this discussion, so why was she egging him on?

Because she needed to know what had happened. And because talking about their past was preferable to wondering if she had a future.

"I left you alone to care for Jacob on your own, at least part of the time. I can't explain why. It's… I didn't handle your hurts very well." He shook his head, the pain in his face deepening. "I'm sorry, and I feel like if I'm going to be staying here for a few days you need to know."

He was apologizing to her? Yeah, he'd trashed her heart and definitely needed to address that, so she was grateful, but… "I started it."

"There was a lot going on then. You were dealing with too many things." Linc's shoulders tightened as though he was gripping the edge of the counter with all of his strength. "You're dealing with a lot now. I need you to know I'm here for you until this is resolved. I'm not going anywhere. I've made sure to be assigned as the liaison between the sheriff and the park service."

I'm here for you. The words fell like gentle rain on dry ground. Tears she hadn't known were waiting at the gate pressed against her eyes.

Her father had died. Owen had decimated her heart. Linc had left her.

Yet, it was as though God was whispering to her heart through Lincoln's words. *I'm here for you.*

"Thank you." Maybe she was talking to Linc. Maybe she was praying out loud. She wasn't really sure, but the sense of peace that overtook her stilled the restlessness in her body and spirit.

Still, she couldn't bring herself to address her own actions on the night he'd walked out of the house. Who she'd been then was so much different than who she was now. She needed some time to adjust before she could make her own apologies.

She settled in and crossed her legs, watching Lincoln, needing to say something. Needing, despite the peace inside of her heart, to do something. "What comes next? I can't stay in the house forever, hiding from whoever is after me." The thought of herself as a target still sent a shudder through her.

Linc hesitated, then rounded the counter and sat on the end of the couch farthest from her. "I want to talk to the protestors. Detectives Blankenship and Majenty spoke to them before we found—" He cleared his throat. "I want to talk to them myself. I'd like for you to come with me."

"Why?"

"To see if you recognize anyone. To look at build, at eyes, to listen to voices, to—"

"He never said anything." Other than the muttered curses

whenever Linc had intervened, her attacker had been silent both times.

A trait that made him twice as terrifying.

"I think the answer lies with the protestors. They've escalated from vandalism. Maybe someone thinks, with you out of the way, they'll get what they want."

"But what about Ellis?" Why not kill her, if they wanted her gone? Lincoln's theory held water, but there were leaks in the bucket.

"Ellis could be unrelated. Look, I could be totally barking up the wrong tree, but we need to at least eliminate the possibility someone outside of your gate has decided to move outside of the law."

Not only outside of the law, but also squarely into murder.

SEVEN

A soft scraping sound reached into Lincoln's subconscious and jerked him awake. He sat straight, dragging numb fingers down his face as he tried to orient himself. His upper back and neck throbbed pain straight into the top of his skull, probably from the way he'd dropped off with his head awkwardly positioned on the sofa.

How had he fallen asleep? Sure, the house alarm was on, so the door chimes would alert him if someone entered, but he'd never fully trusted technology to do the job a vigilant and trained human should do. He'd only sat down for a minute to talk to Angie, then—

The sound came again, softly.

Linc bit back a chuckle and settled in the sofa, as another soft snore drifted from Angie's chair.

It seemed she'd succumbed to sleep as well, her head resting on the back of the oversize chair. He ought to wake her so she wouldn't have a serious pain in her neck, but it was probably too late.

It was definitely too late for him. Gently, he stretched his neck from one side to the other, hoping to alleviate some of the pain.

Who was he kidding? It never really went away. After his run-in with Angie's attacker the day before, there was no way he'd find relief anytime soon. He hated weakness. Hated himself for the momentary lapse in attention that had led to his downfall. If he could have that moment back…

He glanced at Angie, then away. If he could have a lot of moments back, he'd do them so differently.

The windows glowed with morning light, indicating he'd slept for several hours. Sure enough, a glance at his watch showed it was nearly six in the morning.

Across the room, Angie shifted and breathed more quietly, but she didn't wake. It was no surprise. She had to be exhausted after all she'd endured since arriving home from Las Vegas. Losing the grant would have been enough to deal with. But two attacks, a shooting, a murder… No one was superhuman enough to overcome all of that stress quickly, no matter how much Angie wanted to pretend she was okay.

It was no wonder she'd come close to cracking the night before. As she'd paced and shaken her hands, Linc had been taken back several years to the night she'd finally fallen apart during Jacob's recovery. There were times in that season when he'd wondered how much emotion she could hold in before she exploded, and it had taken longer than he'd have ever imagined. The night she'd succumbed to grief and exhaustion, the same caged-animal behavior she'd exhibited last night had risen to the surface, as though the energy pent up inside of her would destroy her if it didn't find release.

Angie didn't like to cry in front of anyone. She didn't like to show weakness. She valued control.

That was something Linc could appreciate.

Still, her behavior the previous night had been more than he could bear. The first time he'd witnessed it, that restless need to move had driven her into his arms, seeking an outlet that wouldn't have been good for either one of them.

Frankly, it had driven him into hers. He could have easily let her lead the way in taking things too far. If he was being totally honest, he had wanted to allow it more than anything in the world.

The alarm bells in his brain had stopped him. The force of his own emotions had shocked him into backing away from her, maybe too abruptly.

For him, that moment hadn't been a simple need to connect in any way that would cover the pain. Something around his heart had snapped and a totally new thing had rushed in through the gaps.

No, he'd realized their late-night talks and their teaming up to help her brother through physical therapy and long, painful days and nights had created a bond between them, one like he'd never felt with another person, not with his army buddies and certainly not with any other woman he'd ever met.

What he'd felt for Angie had been completely different. Whatever had happened between them in those long weeks had made him want something with her that he'd never wanted with another person.

He had realized with a mind-shattering clarity he was falling in love with her.

Not only would his respect for her never let them push across physical boundaries, but his sense of self-preservation also wouldn't let him cross the emotional line.

Overwhelmed by the strain of caring for Jacob and with his heart's new realizations, he'd practically bolted from her embrace, from where he was right now, on this couch.

He could almost see himself standing in the center of this very room, dragging his hands through his hair where her fingers had been, stuttering and stumbling over his words in an effort to explain his actions without explaining himself.

In the end, he'd simply walked away, knowing if he stayed, he'd find himself leading the way down a path they didn't need to follow. He'd packed his bags and fled the house like she was chasing him with a knife.

Maybe she had been, metaphorically, because the next few months had left him feeling as though someone had sliced open his chest and left him to bleed out. He couldn't be alone with her. Couldn't bear to be in the same room with her. Every time he was, he wanted to say things he shouldn't—not to his best friend's sister. Not when their lives were upside down.

He'd taken the coward's way out and offered to "help" by only coming by during the night, when Angie rested. When her mother had arrived, he'd only visited when Angie wasn't home.

Once Jacob was well and was working with him at the NPS, he'd stopped visiting the ranch at all.

It was too much.

He'd missed everything about Angie, and it had taken months for him to convince his heart she'd be better off with someone who wanted a family and a future. He liked his job and his bachelor life, with no one else to worry about, no matter what his heart had tried to tell him.

Now, as she slept, the worry lines that had etched her forehead the day before relaxed. He hadn't realized how deeply they were ingrained until this moment of peace.

Linc looked away. He shouldn't be noticing anything. Not her serenity. Not the way her dark blond hair had straggled out of the ponytail she'd nervously pulled the night before. Not the way everything about her reminded him of what might have been if he hadn't been a coward.

Now he was no longer a coward. He was a broken man. Even his team was moving on without him, possibly catching a case he still knew nothing about. The last thing he wanted was to burden someone, and he was headed that way at breakneck speed. With this injury—

Linc jerked his head to one side as if he could throw off the thoughts, but it drove home the fact that every little movement led to pain.

He stood quietly and walked into the kitchen. This day needed to begin. He needed to be alert if he was going to watch out for Angie.

In the kitchen, he slipped the carafe from the coffee maker and let the water run slowly to avoid waking Angie. Out the window over the sink, the sky was lightening rapidly, a riot of pinks and oranges fading into a blue washed by the previous day's rain.

If only he could wash away the memory of Ellis West's battered body.

He shook his head again, trying to clear it.

A soft sound from the living area told him he hadn't been successful in his attempts at silence. "What time is it?"

When he turned away from the sink, he saw Angie standing at the bar. She'd pulled the band from her hair so it flowed past her shoulders in chaotic, sleep-tossed waves. An air of restful sleep seemed to cling to her.

He turned away. "Where's your coffee?" The words were gruff and clipped. He really didn't need to see her newly awake. It made him start thinking of what it might be like if this was their normal kind of morning, if they shared coffee and conversation on a regular basis as they started their days together.

Angie walked into the kitchen, securing her ponytail, and grabbed a canister from the counter near the coffee maker. She handed it to him then went to sit at the island, seeming content to let him work. "Did you sleep?"

"I did." Linc measured out the coffee, careful not to look at her.

"Good. You needed it more than I did. How's your back?" She sounded genuinely concerned.

"Fine." He clipped that word, too. The sooner he got food into him, the sooner he could down some ibuprofen and hopefully make that true. In the army, he used to choke down those things dry, on an empty stomach. Age and stomach pain had cured him of that habit.

There was a long stretch of silence, broken by what sounded like Angie drumming her fingers on the counter. Finally, she sniffed. "What happens now?"

"With?" He capped the canister and slid it across the counter, then went to the fridge. There was zero desire in him to talk about what came next with his injury, especially since he didn't have any answers. He pulled open the fridge and grabbed the eggs. "Hungry?"

"Not really, but I'll eat whatever you make. There's bacon in the deli drawer if you want some." The light tapping sound continued. "What happens now with the—the…" The words trailed into nothing.

Bumping the fridge door to close it, Linc turned and looked at her. She was staring in the direction of the barn. *The murder.*

He needed to get out of his own stupid head. His little rebound into past feelings was trivial compared to what Angie was dealing with. *This is not about you, Tucker.*

"How much detail do you want?" He set the bacon and eggs on the counter with some cheese from the deli drawer. Was she asking for details about how the coroner would proceed with autopsies? About interviews and testing and all of the minutiae that went with a homicide investigation?

"I mostly want to know what's next for me. You can handle the stuff I don't want to know about." She shredded the edge of a receipt he'd noticed on the counter earlier.

She needed a plan, some direction. That much, he could give her. "Like I said, I want to talk to the protestors, and I'd like you to go with me. Maybe you—"

Her phone vibrated on the counter and she reached for it, frowning at the screen. "It's the contractor. He's on his way over."

"Why?"

"Because he has a job to do." The snap in her words betrayed her anxiety.

"Not today. Have him come straight to the house so you can talk to him, and I'll see if I can get him cleared to work tomorrow. I think the crime-scene unit is finished there."

Unless this continued to escalate.

He couldn't allow that, because if this went any further, then Angie might be the next victim of a killer.

She was tired of being bossed around. Tired of being told what she could do and where she could go on her own property. In the wake of Ellis's death, it was necessary, she understood. Still, the restrictions served to drive the horror of the situation deeper into her mind when all she wanted to do was make it all stop. If she didn't move forward, fear and grief would destroy her.

She texted Carter, then headed for the door to meet him when he pulled in.

Lincoln followed. "You're not meeting anyone alone."

With a huff, she stopped in the middle of the living room. This used to be her safe place, but now Linc was everywhere she looked. With everything else happening, having him in the house felt like the most dangerous threat of all. "It's my contractor, not the Big Bad Wolf."

"Wolves wear sheep's clothing."

She blew out another puff of frustration. "I've met with him alone dozens of times. He and his crew have been working on the property for weeks. They built the original dorm and lab a couple of years ago. I'm pretty sure if he wanted to drag me away, he'd have done it already. He's had more than his share of chances."

Linc followed her onto the porch and stood to the side as Carter Holbert pulled up in his white pickup with *Holbert Construction* splashed across the side in shades of red and orange. Dressed in jeans and a white button-down with the company logo over the right pocket, he was already talking when he stepped out of the truck. Despite the salt-and-pepper in his hair, Carter looked younger than his sixty-plus years. "I figured you'd want to meet down at the ranch." Slamming the truck door behind him, he squinted toward the porch steps, where Angie waited. "Sorry about yesterday. Half of my crew is out with the flu and without Isla..." He cleared his throat, looking pained. "We'd planned to get out here bright and early to get some excavating done, but the park service called. Had an inspector at the Desert View Watchtower yesterday who wasn't a fan of the fencing we put up to keep the public out of the construction zone."

"I had to take care of some things here." She really didn't want to go into detail about her woes. "Has there been any news about Isla?"

The lines in Carter's forehead deepened. "No. I talked to some detectives right after she disappeared, but I haven't heard anything since." Isla had worked for Carter for years, keeping his office running in top condition. She'd always been friendly, though she'd seemed distracted in the weeks leading to her disappearance.

It clearly pained Carter to talk about her, so Angie moved on. "I'm sure restoring a historic structure comes with its own set of headaches." Built in the 1930s, and now housing a gift shop on the ground floor, the tower was a landmark on the South Rim. Conservationists had been working floor-by-floor to preserve the structure. Carter's company had been called in to restore the exterior. The entire site was closed to tourists, and Carter had been under pressure to finish quickly. It had caused multiple delays to the work on the ranch, but now that she was dealing with a money crunch, the delays didn't make her quite so antsy.

Carter walked to the porch and rested one foot on the bottom step. He glanced over at Lincoln. "Carter Holbert." He squinted. "Have we met before?"

"No. I'm a friend of the Garcia family. Lincoln Tucker."

Carter nodded slowly. "Good to meet you." He turned to Angie. "I can get my crew out this afternoon. I need to bring in a few big machines to dig a couple of feet down. You've got enough topsoil here before you hit rock that we can do a crawl space instead of elevating the structure on piers like some of the cabins were built. That'll give you easier access to the plumbing and electrical and give you flexibility for future expansion."

From the quotes, it would also cost more. It was time to swallow her pride and face the facts. "We might need to press Pause for a bit." Not because of Ellis's murder, either.

"Why? I know you're ready to get moving on this next phase." Carter had done all of her renovations and new construction. He knew what the project meant to her. He'd also gone to school with her father. They'd played football together and had been friends until her father's death from cancer while Angie was in college. Ellis's father, Javi, had been killed in a car accident a short time later.

The idea of going into details made her stomach squeeze, so she took the easy route. "We've had a few incidents on the property." Linc hadn't told her how much she could say, so she kept it to a minimum. "Coconino County is investigating and they want some space while they look for evidence."

"They've shut down the job site?"

Linc spoke from behind her. "The construction site isn't involved, but we'd still like to keep traffic to a minimum."

Carter nodded slowly. "I'll hold my crew until you say the word, but is it okay if I head over and look around? I told Mac I'd help dig the trenches for his plumbing. His crew's got the same flu bug that's decimated mine."

"Tomorrow." Linc walked up beside Angie and looked down at Carter. "I'm sure they'll be cleared out by then."

One eyebrow arched, Carter lifted a half smile. There was no telling what he thought was going on between Linc and Angie. "Gotcha. I'll head over to the tower, tell my guys to keep on keepin' on there. With the crew reduced, it'll help not to split them." He dipped his chin and headed for the truck. "Call me when you're ready."

Angie chewed her lower lip. She should be honest about her financial situation, but she didn't want to do it in front of Linc. She looked over at him. "Stay here."

She jogged down the steps and caught up with Carter. "Hey." She kept her voice low and prayed he'd understand her plight.

Carter looked over her shoulder toward the house, then lowered his voice. "You okay? You look a little stressed. Is it…him? You need help?"

The man had no idea, but it wasn't whatever Carter suspected. "No. It's money." Carter would probably drop the project, which meant she'd have to start over getting bids and signing contracts. They were already behind schedule, and with the ranch in the center of a criminal investigation, this could be the end of her dream. She charged ahead. "I lost out on a grant I was counting on. I need to move some things around before I can pay you."

"I see." Carter nodded. He scrubbed his hand along his chin and stared toward the canyon. "Angie, we'll get this done, okay? You've always been good with paying, and I'll work with what your deposit covered until I run out. We'll excavate the site, even if I have to do the digging myself."

His kindness might be what broke her. "Thanks, Carter." He gave her hand a quick squeeze. He stared toward the ranch for a long time, then turned his face toward the sky as though he was reading something in the cirrus clouds that wisped the big blue. "I believe in what you're doing here. My great-grandmother was Hopi, and I want to see that heritage taken care of."

"I know. I can dig into my savings and pay you, which is likely what I'll do, but it leaves me nothing for a rainy day. I was counting on that grant." She'd been so certain.

Carter chuckled softly. "Got a little cocky, did ya?"

Her head jerked back and she looked over her shoulder to see if Linc was listening. He was texting on his phone, pretending not to watch. "I… What?"

"I'm sorry," Carter said quickly, as though speed could erase his original thought. "We've worked together and I knew your dad and all, but not well enough to say that to you." He cleared his throat as he winced. "Sorry."

She'd ignore his mild criticism, though it gnawed at something at the back of her neck. "It's okay."

"What if…? What if I bought the ranch from you?" Before the shock fully registered, he hurried on. "I'll keep you on as a manager, and Rosa, too. And I'll only buy the ranch land, not the land around the house. I've got some saved. Business has been good, and it'll be a tax write-off, if—"

She gasped. "Carter." The pressure from too many decisions and the voices of too many people saying she needed to give up her home exploded in her chest. "The ranch isn't for sale. Not to you. Not to the government. Not to the protestors outside my gate. Not. For. Sale."

He nodded slowly, his expression sympathetic. "I'm sorry. That was a big jump. A lot of what I've said today has been out of line."

"It's okay. I shouldn't have snapped. There's too much going on here."

"Oh. Yeah. I…I wasn't going to say anything, but I ran into the sheriff when I was getting coffee at Misty's. He said they found Ellis West. I'm sorry to hear that."

"Me, too."

"Listen, Angie, you be safe. There's a lot of weird things going on around the area lately. I've heard rumblings about a serial killer or something and—"

"A what?" Angie straightened. A serial killer? Had that been who killed Ellis?

Who was after her?

Was Linc hiding something? "Carter, I have to get moving. Come by anytime after tomorrow morning to work. You've got a gate code—just give me a heads-up." She walked him to the truck and watched as he drove away.

Behind her, the door closed. She stood a long time, staring at the land her family had owned for over a century. Why did everyone suddenly want her to give it up? *God, are You telling everyone else something and not me?*

The response was silence. She went inside to what might be another uncomfortable encounter. Life was full of discomfort and danger.

It was easier to focus on discomfort.

When she walked into the house, Linc was setting plates on the island, but even his bacon, egg and cheese sandwiches couldn't distract her. "A serial killer? There's a *serial killer* out there?"

He froze, holding a plate an inch from the counter. "Where did you hear that?" There was genuine shock on his face. "Is that what the rumor mill has spun up?"

She related Carter's comments, leaving out his offer to buy the ranch. She still hadn't decided if she was shocked, angry or confused.

The plate settled onto the granite counter with a thunk as Linc shook his head. "Not that I know of, but I'll make some calls. It's possible my team knows something and they haven't told…" His expression hardened, and he turned toward the fridge. "Juice?"

Her agitation dropped a few levels. Linc should be with his team, not babysitting her and making her breakfast. If they were truly keeping something from him, that would wound him more than she could imagine.

Angie was grateful for his protective presence, but her gratitude was tinged with guilt. There was nothing she could say to help ease his hurt and frustration. She opted for gratitude. "Thanks for breakfast."

"Yep." He didn't turn as he poured juice. "Eat. We have some protestors to talk to."

His unspoken words hung in the air. *And a killer to find.*

EIGHT

That case Thomas had mentioned in passing... If rumors of a serial killer were flying, then there had to be more to it than Thomas had hinted at.

Linc lifted his foot from the gas pedal and let his truck slow as he neared the gate. Was his team purposely keeping things from him? Or had they simply moved forward without his unnecessary weight?

Not needed. Not wanted. Useless.

He gripped the wheel tighter, dragging his focus to the present. Half a dozen protestors had arrived already. He needed to shove aside his little pity party. Angie's life might depend on it.

Another vehicle approached, probably more people planning to make their desires for Angie's land known.

What did this crew do for a living? Who had time to sit all day long, even for something they believed in? He couldn't remember being still for a moment in his life, at least not after elementary school. He'd worked from the time he was old enough to get a job, had signed up for the army at eighteen and had moved straight from there to the National Park Service. If he wasn't working, what good was he? The only time off he'd ever taken had been to help Jacob recover.

Look where that had landed him.

He hardly dared to look at Angie. *Focus*.

She'd come into the house with fire in her eyes, and it wasn't about the idea of a serial killer on the loose. Whatever Carter had said had upset her, and she wasn't inclined to talk about it.

Interesting.

Linc shifted the truck into Park and killed the engine as the protestors grabbed signs and moved to the sides of the road, preparing for him to drive through their miniature gauntlet.

Surprise, folks. He was staying firmly on his side of the gate.

He studied the crowd. "Didn't you give me a woman's name the other day?" There were no women in the group, just men who appeared to be in their twenties.

"Monica Huerta. She works part-time as a manager at an apartment complex, so she's only here some of the time."

"You're pretty familiar with the protestors?"

Angie shrugged, seeming distracted by the small knot of people. It had to be disconcerting to be the object of an organized campaign bent on misunderstanding her motives. "I know Monica and maybe one or two others by sight. Most are from out of town. They rotate through on a schedule, it seems."

So there were a lot of strangers involved, people unknown to local law enforcement. He'd see about gathering names and running a few federal checks. With the violence on the ranch and the rumors of a killer on the loose, the idea of out-of-towners bent on causing trouble made him antsy.

Reaching for the door handle, Linc watched Angie. "Anybody look familiar?"

Angie chewed her lower lip, a sure sign she was stressed, probably at the idea her attacker could be staring through the truck windows even now. Finally, she shook her head. "No, but he was wearing heavier clothes both times. It all moved so fast…" Her hand fluttered then dropped into her lap. "It could have been anybody."

"I want you to stay in the truck, okay?" Before she could protest, he charged on. "Watch these guys unless I wave you over. I want to see how they react to your presence. See if anybody acts strange when I start talking, or if anyone is overly interested in you and not paying attention to me. Body language says a lot, and you can be my eyes while I'm speaking with individuals." When he was actively working with the team, this was a routine he and Jacob had pulled off naturally. Given Jacob was out of the country, and Linc was currently separated from his team, he would have to improvise.

He shook it off. There were bigger things at play than what his guys were doing without him.

The group of men eyed Linc warily as he approached, but they didn't retreat. Three of them stood quietly along both sides of the road.

When he reached the gate, the approaching car parked by two others in the shade near a stand of trees. Three more men got out, and with curious glances at Linc, they joined the rest of the group, taking signs that were handed to them. All of them watched silently, letting their placards speak for them.

Stop Destroying the Land!

The Canyon Belongs to Everyone!

No More Tourists!

He bit back a sardonic smile. That last one was ironic, given what Angie had said about several of the protestors being from out of state.

The driver of the car exited the vehicle and watched Linc closely, his posture rigid.

Linc kept a careful eye on him.

The guy knew he was under scrutiny. He seemed to deliberately relax as he shut the car door and approached, tossing his keys repeatedly. He walked past the other men, saying hi and smiling as though this was a soiree at the country club. He stopped at the center of the gate and extended his hand toward Linc, who was a few feet away. "Hi. Riley Jeffries."

This guy was slimy. Everything about his demeanor said

he believed he ran the show. This was his club and he was the consummate host.

Disgusting.

Linc ignored the extended hand as he eyed Riley, from his artfully mussed dark hair to his hiking boots. He was wearing gray cargo pants and a green athletic shirt, as though he was about to go hiking in the canyon. Given the extreme differences between Riley's outfit and the clothing of the man who had attacked Angie, there was no way to tell if they were one and the same. The build was similar, but the hooded sweatshirt had distorted true height and weight.

Linc tapped the badge hanging around his neck. "Special Agent Lincoln Tucker, National Park Service Investigative Services."

"Is that an actual thing?" The veiled derision in Riley's voice was acidic.

Lincoln responded, not with fake sugar, but with the law-enforcement equivalent. Humor. "Yeah, we're hoping for our own television show any day now."

The flicker on Riley's face said he wasn't sure whether Linc was being sincere or sarcastic.

Good—this guy needed to be off balance.

He recovered quickly. "Well, man, how can I help you?"

It took a lot of training to stay calm in the face of overwhelming arrogance. Personal feelings couldn't affect Linc's investigative instincts, no matter how much this guy rubbed him the wrong way. "I know the deputies talked to you yesterday, but I wanted to get some clarification, talk to you guys myself." He propped an elbow on the fence and leaned as though they were two guys chatting about the weather. It was taking everything he had not to pull the tough-cop card and put this guy in his place, but that would wound Riley's pride and shut him down. "How late were you all out here yesterday?"

Riley studied the sky as if he could calculate time and date by the position of the sun. More likely, he was buying time. "Not sure what time it was, but when the storm started blowing, we booked. Definitely don't want anyone getting struck by lightning for the cause."

"And what's the cause?"

"You don't know?" Riley arched an eyebrow, and he gestured toward the men behind him, who'd dispersed to the camping chairs in the shade of trees near the cars. "We don't believe in legacy inholdings in the national parks, and we particularly don't agree with continued development on those lands. Angie Garcia and Fairweather Ranch are planning to expand the tourist trade here. Her family has a history of overgrazing the land and running a dude ranch that brought in way too many careless tourists. All of that leads to erosion and endangers the canyon. We want to keep the canyon pristine for future generations and open for everyone to enjoy. No one should own part of our country's natural heritage."

Despite his best efforts, Linc's jaw tightened. Aside from the opinions on inholdings, everything Riley said he wanted fit with what Angie was doing. These guys really were clueless.

Either Riley wasn't being entirely forthcoming, or somebody else was pulling the strings of this protest. They had to know the truth about Angie's plans. She'd publicized everything, had held public fundraisers, and her grant nomination had made the local news.

Yet Riley seemed ignorant.

"I'm with you on keeping public land public." And with returning native lands to tribes, but not taking private land from its owners. Seeming to agree with Riley might open the guy up. "So how did you learn about the new development on the Garcia ranch?"

For a split second, Riley froze, almost as though he'd entered suspended animation. As quick as it happened, his arrogance settled around him again. "It's not like she's kept it a secret. Everyone around town knows."

So he *had* seen the news about what Angie was doing. Riley was either lying about how he'd found out, or he was lying about his understanding of what Angie was working to build.

Linc was pretty sure he was never going to be a fan of Riley Jeffries.

"Anything else?" Riley glanced over his shoulder at his group. "We're due a quick meeting. Want to go over the rules. With the recent happenings on the ranch, I want to make sure our people know trespassing won't be tolerated. And before you ask, I assured the sheriff's detectives the two protestors who did the previous damage have been handled. We turned their names over to the sheriff, and they're no longer welcome with us."

The words weren't spoken with any sort of compassion for Angie. In fact, the speech had the air of a rehearsal.

When Linc had a few minutes, he'd call Detective Blankenship and see if she'd gotten the same verbiage. It was likely she had. "I'm going to need those names."

"You can't ask the sheriff?"

"You're right here in front of me. Lot easier for you to tell me." Riley offered two names, and Linc jotted them down, then jerked his chin toward the men in the chairs. "I want to talk to the rest of the group."

With a bored sigh, Riley shook his head. "I told you. We're about to—"

Linc whistled shrilly. This was getting old and going nowhere. He held up his badge for the protestors to see and waved them closer.

Riley's face was a thundercloud. Gone was the arrogance and condescension. Linc had usurped his authority, and he wasn't happy about it.

Yeah, Riley Jeffries was one to keep an eye on. On the surface, he didn't seem the type to kidnap a woman or beat a man to death, but evil came in all shapes and sizes.

The small group of men gathered around the gate, close enough for Angie to see. None of them paid any attention to the truck, even after Linc turned and made a point of looking in her direction. He asked a few generic questions, then let them go. He could get the rest of what he needed from the sheriff's office, and he wanted to maintain some goodwill in case he had more to ask these guys later.

As he walked to the truck, he replayed the conversation in his head, searching for answers.

That conversation had brought him no closer to finding Ellis West's killer or Angie's attacker, but it had made one thing very clear… The danger to Angie came from multiple angles, and he'd have to be vigilant if he wanted to keep her safe.

He was missing something. The conversation with Riley Jeffries had left him feeling like he was juggling and was about to drop all of the balls. The attacks, the shooting, the protestors, the murder, the mysterious mention of a case but no word from his team…

While Angie talked with Rosa in the house for their morning meeting, Linc had headed for the barn, promising to feed and water Chance while he was there. He needed some time alone to put his thoughts in order, and he certainly thought more clearly when Angie wasn't in the room.

The horse had been reluctant to trust Linc at first, standing at the back corner of the stall when Linc entered. Chance wasn't combative or afraid, just wary. After realizing Linc was the key to food and fresh water, though, the horse warmed up considerably.

When Linc set the bucket of water on the floor, a warm weight rested on his shoulder. A slightly damp puff blew across his ear.

So Chance was a snuggler? He hadn't seen that coming.

Linc allowed himself a smile as he scratched the horse's muzzle. "You lonely out here, buddy?"

Chance huffed as though he recognized that Linc understood.

"Yeah, you're used to a barn full of other horses who work like you do." Though other things had taken precedence, they should probably move him back to the main ranch barn. The horse likely also missed his rider. While Chance belonged to Fairweather Ranch, Ellis had been the one he'd bonded with, according to Rosa and one of the other ranch hands Linc had spoken to the day before. It was an accepted fact around the property that Chance and Ellis were buddies.

Given how he'd been found saddled and tied to the fence, there was no telling where he'd been between the time of Ellis's disappearance and the attack on Angie. Chance's reappearance near the barn brought up more questions.

Ducking his shoulder slightly, Linc turned and faced the horse, scratching his neck as he searched the animal's eyes. "What did you see out there? Where were you for an entire day? And who tied you to the fence?" If only the horse could answer. Had the attacker simply stumbled upon Chance on the property and seen an opportunity to draw out Angie? Or had he taken the horse at the same time as Ellis and held him somewhere, hoping to use the animal to get to Angie?

Yeah, if this animal could talk, they could probably apprehend their killer and close this case by nightfall. "Too bad you never learned English, huh?"

Linc's phone buzzed in his pocket.

Chance tossed his head and backed away at the slight sound, then nudged Linc out of the way and started slurping water.

Guess that conversation was over.

With one more pat to the horse's neck, Linc left the stall and latched it, then checked the screen before answering.

"Thomas." He walked across the aisle and leaned against the same stall door he'd used to hold himself up the day before. At least now his pain level had dropped to a three so he could function. "Thanks for calling me so quickly." He'd texted a few minutes earlier, knowing Thomas would call when he was free.

"I'm headed to a possible crime scene, and thought I'd give you an update while I'm on the road."

Linc's eyes shut tight. If he wasn't sidelined now, he'd be headed out, too, tracking down evidence and searching for answers with his team by his side. "What's happening?" His throat was tight, and the words squeezed out with a measure of pain.

"Remains in the woods near Widforss Trail."

"New or old?" Deadly things happened in the canyon. As peaceful and beautiful as it was, danger lurked, both from the natural world and from men plotting evil. Nature often revealed the dead who'd passed centuries earlier alongside the ones who'd passed on more recently. If his team had been called in, the probability was high it was a recent death.

"I won't know how recent until I get there." The click of a turn signal filled the brief silence. "You can't be calling about that because I just hit the road. You need to brainstorm about the West homicide?"

That wasn't his original intention, but bouncing things off Thomas might help untangle the spaghetti in his head. "It's the horse."

"Tell me the horse isn't hurt." Thomas's voice took on an edge he reserved for people who harmed animals and children.

While death and pain were always tragic, when it came to animals and kids, hearts were especially soft. "Chance is fine, but he's missing his rider." He ran down his brief set of questions, hoping Thomas would see something he didn't.

Silence rode the line as Thomas drove. The man was quieter than Linc and Jacob—friendly, but fond of his personal space and protective of his time off-duty with his wife and toddler daughter. He thought deeply and tended to see angles Linc's overthinking and Jacob's rush to action missed.

Finally, Thomas spoke. "If he was still saddled, I'm inclined to believe the bad guy found him wandering and took a chance. I saw you sent his tack in for printing and DNA testing, so maybe something will come from that."

"I'm not sure the horse was wandering. He's lived on Fairweather for years and has only been stabled in the ranch barn."

"So why was he by the house instead of heading for his own stall?" Thomas sighed. "And where was he all day? Better yet…you found West's phone near the barn, correct?"

Thomas's train of thought barreled right through Linc's suspicions. "If Ellis had returned to the ranch, he'd have either stabled his horse or tied him near the cabin. Chance was in neither place."

"You've got an odd one on your hands."

Linc dragged his hand down his face. He needed a whiteboard or a giant piece of paper to start connecting all of his thoughts. "Keep thinking. Maybe something will trigger in that brain of yours."

"Or yours."

True. It was wild how often his subconscious worked through things when he wasn't even trying.

"So was that the only reason you called?" The question was weighted with something hard to read.

Guilt? Linc didn't want to sound like he was whining, but he did want to know what was going on with his team. "You mentioned a case yesterday. I was following up. And then, yeah, I had another question."

"What's your question and then I'll tell you about the case. Yours is probably shorter than mine."

"Doubtful." Still, Linc quickly outlined who Carter was and what he'd said.

"Where would he get the idea there's a serial killer out there? Is that something we're tracking?" Even though Linc wasn't in the field, he was still the team leader, even if Thomas was acting in his place. He should be read in on everything. That he wasn't was painful.

"Interesting."

Linc switched the phone to his left ear. What was Thomas putting down that he wasn't picking up?

"The FBI reached out to us early yesterday. Seems a woman went missing a couple of weeks ago, and she works for Carter Holbert."

So that was what Angie had been asking about when she mentioned a woman's name. "Isla or something?"

"Isla Blake."

"When were you planning to tell me?" There was a kicked-dog bite to the words. His team was shutting him out, realizing his powerlessness to do anything of value for them. Gripping the phone tighter, he tried to ignore the pain of tension piercing his back.

"Hold your literal horses, Tucker." The low hum over the line died away. Thomas had likely reached his destination and shut off the engine of his park-service SUV. "I don't know yet if anything is going on, and the FBI just reached out. They're concerned a serial killer has gone active again."

"Which one?" Arizona had been home to several serial killers, as had multiple national parks across the nation. Unsolved murders and missing persons were plentiful around the Grand Canyon, but none had come across the wire to him lately.

"About a decade ago, there was a rash of seven disappearances around this area. No bodies were found, but it's highly likely, and assumed, that the women are dead."

"I remember that. Seven women vanished, no linking characteristics to them, ranging in ages from seventeen to forty-eight. Differing heights, hair colors, body types, locations—"

"Yep. The only connecting factor was they were all talking to a man online, though he could never be traced because he used the browser on a different burner phone with each of them in order to talk to them online. All drew money from their bank accounts at ATMs, and cameras showed them under some duress as they did, though no one was seen with them. They disappeared with any papers that could identify them, from birth certificates to social-security cards. One woman, Claire Foley, even took hers out of a safe-deposit box a couple of days before she disappeared."

"I remember. About a week after they vanished, their families received their driver's licenses sealed in plastic bags and covered in their blood."

Thomas exhaled loudly. "Yep."

"The FBI thinks Isla Blake was taken by this guy who hasn't made a move in a decade?"

"Isla Blake didn't show up for work after going on a date with a guy she met online. Last sign of movement from her was the use of her ATM card around midnight, at an isolated convenience store outside Williams. FBI is working on getting the footage. Two days ago, her driver's license showed up at the house, covered in her blood. It was slow to get there because the zip code was obscured. Mohave County recognized the MO and contacted the FBI, who had Isla's sister check her files at home. Both her birth certificate and her social-security card are gone."

Linc closed his eyes and exhaled slowly. "Wow."

"It gets worse. The FBI got a call yesterday from the police chief in Williams. A little over a week ago, a twenty-nine-year-old woman disappeared after meeting a guy online—ATM, missing papers and all."

"That's too specific to be coincidence." So a decade later, a killer had returned? What if he'd come after Angie?

But no, nothing about the attacks on Angie or about Ellis West's murder fit the profile.

"These remains we're checking out with the FBI could be one of those two women. We also have a couple of recent missing hikers, so I don't know what to add until I get there."

"I assume Carter Holbert was questioned and cleared?"

"He was. He had an alibi for his missing office manager, and nothing points to him."

At least he had a little bit of good news. "Who's the other missing woman?" His phone buzzed, and he glanced at the screen. While the number wasn't one saved in his phone, he recognized it from earlier in the day. Now was the worst possible time, but he couldn't leave the call unanswered. "Hang on. I have to take another call, but keep me posted."

"You, too. Let me know if you need anything. We'll do what we can."

He was sure they'd help where they could, but his team was moving forward without him.

And it was all because of phone calls like the one he was about to take—the one that could change his life forever.

NINE

She'd never felt so exposed in her life.

Angie glanced around the radiology waiting room at Flag-staff Medical Center and tried not to shrink.

She was not a person who shrank.

They'd called Linc back for his MRI nearly an hour earlier, after a whirlwind rush to make the ninety-minute drive to Flag-staff. He'd received the call about a cancellation and had rushed into the house like a tornado, scaring her half to death before she figured out why he was in such an agitated state.

The last thing she'd wanted to do was leave the ranch to make the trip to Flagstaff. She'd argued.

He'd countered.

She'd finally given in. No amount of reminding him she knew how to protect herself, or that Rosa and two other ranch hands were nearby, could dissuade him. *Look what's happened already with everyone around. You think it's going to get better?*

Clearly, he didn't believe it would. He'd been hypervigilant the entire drive, fidgety even for Linc.

Well, she was fidgety, too. No matter what games she played or books she opened on her phone, she couldn't escape the feeling someone was watching her.

She scanned the room, but no one seemed to be paying her any undue attention. A handful of people were waiting in the small space, and most were absorbed in their phones or in quiet conversations with companions.

Well, she couldn't sit still any longer.

Angie stood and walked to the entrance of the waiting room, then stepped into the hall, running her hands down the seams of her jeans. The gesture made her look as antsy as she felt, but she couldn't stop herself.

Medical facilities set her teeth on edge. The smells. The sounds. Even though Jacob's treatment had largely been at the VA hospital in Las Vegas after he was transferred from Texas, all hospitals were cut from the same cloth.

Being here brought back the intensity of her fear and stress in those long days and weeks of her brother's recovery. It was bad enough Linc had been beside her pretty much twenty-four hours a day since she'd been attacked, but dumping a hospital visit into her lap on top of it? Even for a simple MRI?

Leaning against the wall, she turned her eyes toward the ceiling and squeezed them shut. *Really, God? It's not enough I lose the grant to Owen. It's not enough I have protestors at my door and masked men trying to take me, and a murdered employee. And Linc. Now this?*

Why was He bringing back every single worst moment of her life? *If this is some kind of test, I'll give You the answers You're looking for. Just make it stop.*

"It's tough going through the hard stuff, huh?"

Angie's eyes popped open, and she jerked her head toward the sound, using all of her restraint not to take a defensive swing at the male voice.

"Sorry." A young man, probably college age, stepped back and held up his hand. "I didn't mean to scare you. You looked…" He balled his fists, tensed his shoulders and scrunched his face, then relaxed and smiled. "You looked kind of like that."

She could have taken offense at the characterization, but

he wasn't wrong. The tension in her shoulders and jaw spoke to the truth. "It's okay. I could use the distraction."

"We all could." He leaned against the wall about a foot away and shoved his hands into his pockets. Studying his canvas shoes, he twisted his mouth to one side. "One thing I can pretty much promise you is none of us want to be here." He glanced at her. "Family or friend? Or yourself?"

How would she characterize Linc? He wasn't her family. Three days ago, she wouldn't have called him a friend. But the way they'd talked over the past twenty-four hours… The way she was sweating his test results as much as she was her own safety… The way he'd started taking over her thoughts…

That might be a bridge too far. "A friend. You?"

"My mom. She finished chemo and radiation, and this is her first set of scans after, to see how it worked. The waiting is the worst."

"It really is." At least Linc wasn't waiting to hear if he was going to live or die.

Or was he? For Linc, the job was everything. If he couldn't be a hard-charging federal agent any longer, he'd see it as a kind of death.

Like her and the ranch. If she didn't get things moving soon…

But there were bigger things at play in this moment than her dreams. "Tell you what, I'll pray she gets good news."

"Thanks." The young man offered a smile that seemed to come from somewhere deep inside. "And I'll pray for good news for you, too. Although my mom has said all along she doesn't call the shots here. God does. She keeps texting me that verse in the Bible about how what we suffer here doesn't compare to what God's got for us once we get to Heaven. I'm trying to remember. It's hard, but I'm trying."

Angie turned away to look up the hall. The words landed

hard against her heart. Was she thinking of this in God terms? Or in human terms?

"I'll be honest." The young man straightened and stepped into the middle of the hall. "Another thing." He balled his fists and scrunched his face. "Holding it all? Trying to make it go away? It's not good for you. Eventually, you explode. I learned the hard way. You've got to take things as they come, let the feelings rock you before they settle. Otherwise… Boom." He threw his hands into the air to mimic a bomb.

How well she knew. The night hers had volcanically erupted, feelings had cost her a friend and her peace of mind. She frowned. But had she learned?

"I see you're thinking, so my work here is done." The man smiled as he backed up the hall. "It was good talking to you. I've got to grab a coffee so it'll be nice and hot when Mom gets out. It's her reward for dealing with an MRI. She hates them." He waved, pivoted on one heel and strode up the hall as though he was familiar with the journey.

He probably was, if his mother had already walked the road of diagnosis and treatment.

Life could turn so quickly. All of the plans in the world could fall to pieces in an instant. Jacob had nearly been killed by an IED. Her father had died of cancer. Instant change.

But cancer… It sort of made the chaos around her feel a little less urgent.

Not much less, but a little.

Angie said a quick prayer for the young man's mother and vowed to pray whenever the woman and her son came to mind.

She stared at the wall across from her, letting his words sink in. Was she repeating the mistakes of her past?

Gnawing her bottom lip, she considered her midnight drive from Vegas, how she'd spewed anger but not allowed disappointment to touch her. How she'd pressed her spine into the wall when bullets flew and forced her fear into a dark closet, focusing on what she could do over what she felt. How she'd turned her energy into caring for Chance rather than falling apart in terror in front of Linc.

The truth crashed against her. She was hiding. Burying her emotions. Taking one step, then another, then another, in an effort to outrun them. Focusing on action over feeling.

The practice had made her numb. When was the last time she'd felt joy?

Her eyes slipped closed and she leaned heavily against the wall. She couldn't remember. In burying the fear and the anger, she'd buried the good as well.

The last time she'd squashed her emotions, they'd destroyed what might have been with Linc. Tucking away the negatives also meant she'd hidden anything good she might be feeling toward him.

Things her heart said she was starting to feel again. Things that might never have gone away.

Something in her heart shifted, as though a crack had opened, ushering in a sliver of light. If she allowed herself to feel the fear she'd been burying, was it possible she'd also feel lo—

"Hey."

Her hand flew to her chest as she whipped toward the voice, heart racing.

Linc stood outside the entrance, an eyebrow arched in question. "You were deep in thought."

Something warm and heady rushed from her heart to her fingertips at the sight of him, tall and strong and… And Linc. For a heartbeat, she considered rushing to him, throwing her arms around him and…

And what?

That had happened once before, and he'd pushed her away. There was no way to explain how this was different. If she reached for him again, it would be because he was Linc, not because she was lost and afraid.

"Ang?" He tilted his head. "You okay?"

Exhaling through pursed lips, she wrestled her heart into submission and found her voice. "Good thing we're in a hospital. You nearly gave me a heart attack." She wasn't ready to talk about the thoughts running through her mind. They were too raw, too fragile to expose to the air. "Are you finished already?"

"Already?" He stepped into the hall and motioned for her to walk beside him. They headed for the main entrance. "I was in that metal tube for approximately eight days." He offered an overexaggerated shudder. "Never been a fan of small spaces. I recited every Bible verse I knew and sang every top-forty song since the year 2000."

Angie laughed as they stepped into the sunlight, shoving her feelings into the closet, where they belonged. She couldn't think of them now. "You put on quite a show, huh?" She could sympathize. A knee injury had sidelined her college-basketball career. The worst moments had come in the MRI. It wasn't an experience she wanted to repeat.

Linc tapped his temple. "All in my head, but it was an amazing display of talent."

"I'm sure. Did they tell you anything?"

"No." When the parking lots had been full, they'd parked on top of the parking garage, both seeming to prefer the open space to the enclosed structure. Once they stepped into the shadows, Linc opened the door to the stairs and ushered her in. "They'll send the results to my doctor. She's booked me an appointment for late this afternoon."

Angie stopped on the second landing and faced him one step below her, putting them eye-to-eye. "You took me to the hospital this morning with you, so I'm assuming I'll be along for this visit as well?" Linc shouldn't be alone to face news he might not want to receive.

Some of the tension around his mouth eased. His gaze

locked on to hers, shifting as though he was trying to read her thoughts through her eyes.

Angie let him. Whatever he needed…

Suddenly, time raced backward to before she'd nearly driven them a step too far. Before everything had been awkward and strained between them. When their easy friendship had been shifting into something more.

Into something she'd desperately wanted.

Could they…? Should they…?

Above them, a door crashed closed.

Linc's head snapped toward the sound, breaking the connection. He gripped the handrail tighter, then shook his head.

Angie fought to keep from melting in humiliation. She'd nearly done it again. Had led him down a path they shouldn't have gone down, one he clearly had no interest in walking.

Before she could speak, another door slammed below them.

Linc stepped beside her, drawing her to his side.

A zip of fear ran through her.

From above and below, footsteps approached.

They were caught in the middle, with nowhere to run.

Linc eased Angie closer to the wall. He stepped in front of her, trying to watch the stairs below and above at the same time.

It was probably nothing, but in their current situation, taking chances was out of the question.

He wanted to bang his head against the wall. A wise man would have taken the elevator and avoided being trapped in a stairwell, but he'd had enough of enclosed spaces for one day. He'd made a rookie mistake.

There was no time for self-recrimination now, though.

Reflexively, his hand went to his hip, but his sidearm wasn't there. He had secured it in the vehicle because he had no way to lock it up in the hospital while he was getting his MRI.

He stepped to the side, prepared to shield Angie against whatever came. Likely it was two other people avoiding the elevator.

He prayed that was so. Otherwise, they were about to go to war.

This is what he got for letting her steal his attention. The care in her voice as she'd looked him in the eye and offered to stand beside him… He hadn't realized how much he'd craved connection with her. It was like being lost in the canyon in blistering heat and getting a cool drink of water. Her concern had washed over his soul in a way he couldn't put into words except to say he'd missed her.

He'd been oblivious to everything else in the world, wanting nothing more than to close the two-inch gap between them and—

The footsteps drew closer in both directions. Any second now, people would appear.

If they were bad actors, the only way out was to fight.

The person coming down the stairs appeared first. Running shoes. Black leggings with a bright pink stripe. A T-shirt above the waist. A blond ponytail bopping in time with whatever was playing in the earbuds in the young woman's ears. She appeared to be a college-age kid.

But appearances could be deceiving. She was slightly out of place in the parking garage, seeming to belong more in the gym or on a track. And she was approximately the same age as the protestors who'd been hounding the ranch.

Lincoln tensed, preparing for a confrontation, but the young woman barely seemed to notice them as she passed on the landing, her nose buried in her phone.

He didn't allow himself to relax.

She hardly stepped aside as she passed a man coming up the stairs. His head appeared first, dark hair peppered with gray. A dress shirt and tie. Pressed slacks. A hospital ID hung around his neck.

Lincoln fought the urge to relax. An identification badge meant nothing. It could have been stolen.

The man's gaze caught Linc's as he approached, and he saw Angie tucked into the corner. The man slowed and stopped halfway up the stairs, concern knitting his eyebrows together. "Is everything okay?" He tried to see around Linc to Angie, pale blue eyes seeming to be concerned for her welfare.

Here was the catch… Did Linc continue to stand wary guard against the possible threat, even though he looked like a predator who'd cornered his prey? Or did he defend himself against the idea he was somehow the bad guy? If this guy was innocent and he called Security, they could have big problems. But if Linc let down his guard and this guy was on the hunt, it could sign Angie's death warrant.

"I'm fine." Angie's voice came over his shoulder, though she didn't move from behind him. "I hate elevators, but I'm also creeped out by stairwells. Too many true-crime podcasts." Her chuckle actually sounded authentic.

The man nodded slowly, his gaze roaming the two of them. He hesitated when he saw Linc's badge, which was clipped to his belt. Pausing, the guy nodded slowly, his expression clearing. "Understandable." Keeping to the side of the landing farthest from Angie and Linc, he passed and headed up the stairs. "Be safe." His feet retreated toward the next landing, and Linc nearly sagged against the wall.

Well, against Angie, who was still behind him. Given that his awareness of how close he'd come to kissing her was still zipping through his veins despite the scare, he really didn't need to touch her right now.

"Can't say that wasn't an aerobic workout." Angie eased from behind him and put some distance between them. "My heart's definitely run through a good cardio session. Is it safe to go up now?"

Everything about her was false, from the stilted words to

the high-pitched tone they were spoken in. Either she'd been rattled by the threat…

Or she'd been as affected by the emotion between them as he had.

Dare he hope? Or did he assume she'd read his thoughts about kissing her and was shoving him away?

He huffed out his exasperation. Once again, he was distracted by her. His main job was to get her to the ranch safely, then to discover who had killed Ellis and was out to harm her. Everything else needed to stay locked away.

"Let's go." Ushering her to walk beside him, he headed up the stairs as she matched him step for step. "I'm not a fan of being in this space for much longer. I want to get you home." The sooner she was in a secure location, the better he'd feel.

It had been a mistake to bring her with him. He should have left her with Rosa and the ranch hands, but the thought of having her out of sight for too long had left him uneasy. Later, he'd have to address the deep-seated belief that no one else could protect her as well as he could.

Arrogance like that got people killed.

Especially since, the way his neck and back were throbbing with the tension of the morning and the odd position he'd had to lie down in for the scans, he wasn't so certain he could protect her, either.

They stepped through the metal door into the bright, midday Arizona sunlight. He squinted against the brilliance and paused to acclimate, blinded as his eyes adjusted.

A shadow moved to the right.

Angie screamed.

A blow to the back of his knees rocked him forward and dropped him hard to the concrete.

TEN

"Linc!" Angie's throat ached as his name ripped out in a hoarse shout. Linc dropped hard onto his knees and pitched forward, catching himself before his head hit the concrete.

A man wielding a tire iron spun toward Angie. His face was covered with a bright orange mask. A blue knit cap hid his hair. Dark brown eyes glared a malevolent threat.

A red sedan waited feet away, the driver's-side door hanging open and the engine running.

Not again. Not this again.

She should run, but she couldn't leave Linc, who was struggling to his feet. If the man swung that tire iron at his back, it could paralyze him.

She had to protect him, even if it cost her everything.

At the sound of Linc's movement, the man hesitated, turning away from her. He raised the tire iron, prepared to deal what could be a horrific injury to Linc's upper back.

How did he know where to strike to deal the worst injury to Linc? Or was it simply the most strategic spot to land a blow?

She could not stand by and watch this man destroy him. Without considering the possible consequences, Angie dove. She tucked her shoulder and ran straight into the assailant's side, tumbling them sideways against the door to the stairs. The door held, and the man grunted but managed to stay on his feet.

He dropped the tire iron, wrapped his arms around Angie

and steadied himself. Using the door for leverage he shoved her toward the waiting car, obviously determined to push her into the vehicle and make his escape.

Linc rolled to his side and rose as Angie kicked and flailed. This was not happening. Not on her front porch in the dark of night and not on the roof of a parking garage in broad daylight.

Planting her foot against the car's rear door, Angie shoved backward, spinning them sideways as Linc lunged forward and grabbed her attacker's jacket, jerking him off his feet.

As Angie wrenched away from him and stumbled to safety, a siren suddenly screeched.

A police car accelerated toward them across the open roof, lights whirling as the siren screamed.

The man turned one way and then the other, seeming to judge if he had a way of escape. Finally, he lifted his hands. "I surrender. I'm not armed."

Just like that, he morphed from a horrifying assailant to a quaking coward.

He kneeled and laced his fingers behind his head as the police car came to a stop beside them. "I know how this works. I'm unarmed. I swear."

Mouth hanging open in shock, Linc stared down at their attacker.

Angie backed against the stairwell door. This had to be a trick. The man who'd come at her at the house hadn't shown any signs of backing down. Maybe he knew he was cornered? Could this be over so easily?

A police officer exited his vehicle, hand on his pistol. "What's going on here?"

Linc raised both hands, but he aimed one finger toward his waist. "I'm a federal agent."

Reflexively, Angie raised her arms as well. Her heart pounded against her chest, as though it had remembered how to beat after being frightened into submission.

The officer glanced at Linc and nodded, motioning for him to lower his hands, then looked down at the kneeling suspect. He kept his hand on his pistol as he glanced at Angie. "You okay? We got a call from one of the docs about a man possibly assaulting a woman in the stairwell. I was headed over when I saw your altercation. Figured the siren would put a quick end to things."

Angie said a silent prayer of thanks for the fast-thinking officer and for the suspicious doctor in the stairwell who was the reason for their salvation. If she could find him, she'd thank him repeatedly for being paranoid. She'd even bake him a cake. "I'm fine. That was us. Special Agent Tucker was protecting me. This guy, though?" Angie lowered her hands and pointed at the masked assailant. "I have no idea who he is."

"But he definitely assaulted me and tried to kidnap her." Linc addressed the police officer while keeping one eye on the bad guy.

The officer moved swiftly to cuff the man and to haul him to his feet, then he nodded to Lincoln. "Want to do the honors of unmasking him?"

As Lincoln stepped forward, hysterical laughter bubbled in Angie. She swallowed it, and it went down in a painful lump. Somehow, this felt like the ending of a Scooby-Doo episode, as though they were going to reveal the masked man was her long-lost great-uncle, or Carter the Contractor, or Rosa the Ranch Foreman.

But it was none of them.

Linc stepped back, the mask dangling from his fingers, his glare ice-cold as he stared at the protestor who'd seemed to be in charge earlier. Linc's jaw was tight, and he clenched his fists as though it was all he could do to hold in his anger. He looked at the police officer. "This man, supposedly, is Riley Jeffries. He organized a protest outside of the ranch Ms. Garcia owns."

"I wasn't going to hurt her." Riley's eyes darted from the

police officer to Linc. Gone was the swagger he'd displayed earlier in the day. A scared little boy remained in his place, shaking in the face of authority. "I really wasn't."

"No?" Linc widened his stance and crossed his arms, leveling a hard gaze on the younger man. "You hit me with a tire iron."

Riley's head shook back and forth in denial. "No. I mean, yes. But in the back of the knee, not where it would actually injure you. I just wanted to knock you down."

"And then hit him in the back?" The words raced out before Angie could stop herself.

For the first time, Riley looked at her. "No. I wouldn't have hit him again. Not hard."

"Kidnapping is a serious offense." Linc exhaled loudly and motioned his head toward the officer's patrol car. "Get him out of my sight, please. We'll come by the station and make a statement." He reached into Riley's car and shut off the engine, then passed the keys to the officer.

"Really." Riley jerked and the officer's grip on him tightened. "I was just trying to scare her. We know from the sheriff's questions what happened at the ranch and we thought…" His shoulders sagged. "We wanted to scare you into selling. That's all."

That's all? Angie startled. Terrifying her into believing her life was in danger was a *that's all*? And Ellis… Had they killed Ellis in some failed attempt to frighten her? Her stomach roiled. "You beat a man to death."

"No!" Riley's head shook again. "No. We had nothing to do with anything on the ranch. Today's the first time any of us have laid a hand on you. What happened to that man, we weren't involved. I swear."

"We'll see." Linc handed Riley's mask and cap to the police officer, then hesitated, cocking his head to one side. "You keep saying *we*. *We* followed. *We* didn't do anything. You have an accomplice here today." He looked over his shoulder at the stairway door. "The woman in the workout gear. She was with you. She let you know it was us headed up the stairs and there was someone walking ahead of us. She was texting you when she passed, wasn't she?" He gave the officer a description of the woman. "There may be more. Don't trust this guy. He looks innocent, but this is the fourth attack on Ms. Garcia in a few days, and there was a man murdered on her property. I'm not buying it wasn't him."

Riley nearly whimpered as the officer tugged him toward the car. He protested his innocence the whole way, claiming an alibi. He was yelling frantically when the officer shut the door and walked back, then handed Linc and Angie business cards. "I'll take him straight in and you two can follow. We'll take care of having his car impounded, too." He pointed toward the corner of the roof. "I'll have our guys pull camera footage to seal the deal on this guy."

"Thanks." Linc glanced at the card then pocketed it. "We'll be right behind you."

After the officer pulled away, Angie sagged against the door. With the threat removed, her hands were shaking and her knees had lost their strength. Her heart might never return to a normal rhythm. "I don't understand. This was all done by the protestors? Why would they kill Ellis? It doesn't make any sense."

"No, it doesn't." He reached for her hand and drew her to him, pulling her into a too-brief hug before releasing her. He grabbed her hand to tug her to the car. "That's why we have to get out of here."

Angie forced herself to follow, although she wanted to curl into a ball on the concrete and make herself as small as possible. Or she wanted to beg Linc to hold her until the terror passed. He was moving her too quickly across the parking deck for her to do either. It was all she could do to keep from tripping over her feet. "This isn't over, is it?"

Linc's expression was grim. "Not by a long shot."

There were no protestors at the gate when they returned to the ranch.

Linc punched in a code Angie gave him and they drove through. He watched the gate close behind them. "I'm guessing, now that Riley is talking, we won't see them again."

It hadn't taken long for the police to get Riley to open up, especially when he learned they'd also picked up his girlfriend, Skyler Cliff, waiting in her car in the parking garage for Riley to text her their next move.

For all of his swagger at the gate earlier, Riley had collapsed like a kite in a thunderstorm. While the protestors were a mix of out-of-towners and locals, the catalyst had come from something entirely different.

An anonymous user had posted on a message thread on an environmental website that they'd pay a group to protest the "development" at Fairweather Ranch, so his suspicion had been right. Someone else was pulling the strings.

Following the money might lead to who was coming after Angie. At the very least, it would lead to an interesting conversation with the backer. His team was already on the hunt, tracking the finances and the IP addresses of the person who'd made the offer. It could take hours or days, but at least it was a lead.

Angie shifted in her seat, but she didn't turn her head. She'd been staring out the passenger window for the past half hour, watching the sun sink lower. The way the clouds were streaming in from the west, the sky would be a riot of oranges and reds when the sun set in a little over an hour, lighting fire to the burnished landscape. It was his favorite time of day.

Or it had been. Now he dreaded the darkness that followed.

Approximately twenty-four hours earlier, they'd found Ellis West's body. Five hours earlier, he'd thought it possible they'd found the man's killer.

Three hours earlier, he'd been convinced they hadn't. As much as he wanted this to be over, the uncertainty and the danger dragged on. Their lead wouldn't save Angie if her assailant struck again before they could find answers.

This had to be wearing on her, because it was chewing him up. The day had been far too long, and he'd had to push back his doctor's appointment to the next morning. Answers would have to wait. Angie's safety came first. "What are you thinking over there?"

She shrugged. "Wondering why someone would pay a bunch of college kids from Rhode Island to protest my ranch." She dragged her finger along the window ledge. "Why is this happening to me?" She chuckled, but the sound held no joy. "I'm having a pity party, to be honest."

"Well, if anyone deserves one, it's you. I'll even buy you the cake and candles."

This time, her laugh was genuine. "Thanks. At least you didn't offer me cheese with my 'whine.'"

He smiled, then turned his gaze to the road. As much as she'd had to endure over the past couple of days, she deserved some time to ask the *why* question.

"Hey." Angie leaned forward as they neared the house, squinting toward the ranch out of sight beyond several stands of trees. "Would you mind if we run over to the ranch? Carter said he was going to do some excavating today, and I'd a lot rather go see how that looks than hole up in the house. The sunset will be pretty epic from there, too."

He lifted his foot from the gas as he neared the turn-off for the house. The ranch was fairly wide open, so he'd see if anyone was coming after them. He could keep her shielded from any potential sniper, and they'd be safely in the house before dark settled.

Although the hands were out with the cattle, Rosa was there, so they'd have some form of backup. As much as he hated having Angie in the open, the request made sense. She was bound to feel caged, and it wasn't like she'd asked to gallop off to the canyon alone or something.

He moved his foot to the gas pedal. "We can do that." It would give him another chance to see if they'd missed anything that might relate to Ellis's murder. Then, when they returned to the house, he'd call Thomas. There had been a couple of missed calls from him earlier, when they were at the police station, but Linc was reluctant to talk to him about a possible serial killer in front of Angie until he had more details.

When they parked near Ellis's cabin, Linc held his arm out in front of Angie. "Wait here. Let me scout around to be sure we're clear."

She sat back with a huff. Tough to say if it was frustration, fear or exhaustion.

He could sympathize.

Linc made a quick check of the area, keeping one eye on the truck. He let up on his surveillance when Rosa stepped out of her cabin and walked to the vehicle. The ranch manager carried a pistol at her hip, likely to ward off snakes, but it was wise with all that was happening.

She tossed a wave in his direction, then spoke to Angie through the passenger window.

When he was satisfied the area was as safe as it could be, he motioned for Angie to join him on the far side of the cabin. Behind the crew cabins, a large rectangular pit had been dug, a little over a foot deep. It looked as though Carter was planning to put a crawl space beneath the dormitory to provide for easier access to ductwork and pipes instead of raising the structure off the ground like some of the others on the property.

Rosa and Angie joined him, and Angie studied the excavation. She looked over her shoulder at Rosa. "He got a lot done today."

"Yep. Said once his crew is healthy, he'll get them out here full-time."

Angie frowned. She was probably wondering how she'd pay for the work without dipping into her savings.

Rosa leaned her shoulder against Angie's. "He said he'd work out funding with you, but he believes in what's happening here. His great-grandmother was Hopi. Let him help you out. You've run this place on donors for years. If he wants to be one of them…"

Angie's smile was tight. There was something else going on, but Linc couldn't read what it was.

He paced the perimeter, eyeing the work. A number of smaller trenches ran off from the main site, several feet in every direction. "What are these? Do you know, Rosa?"

Angie joined him. "I might know. Carter was helping one of the subcontractors by digging where they're going to run pipes and drains."

Made sense.

"He took the dirt from the excavation over to that spot behind the barn and evened out the ground so we can enclose a paddock later. Said to consider it a favor."

"That was nice." Angie jumped into the hole, which came to below her knees, and Rosa joined her. They wandered the space, pacing off rooms and discussing their vision.

Planting her boot heel, Angie dragged a line down the center of the excavation. "If the hallway is here, then—" She stumbled, and Rosa reached out to steady her. Rotating her ankle, Angie inspected the heel of her boot. "Rock."

Linc jumped in and headed toward her, eyeing the ground. "You okay?" While the topsoil was a bit deeper here at the edge of the forest than it was in other areas of the canyon, it still didn't take much digging to get down to solid rock.

"Yeah. I caught my heel on…" Angie trailed off, then kneeled, swiping gently at something in the dirt. "It's not rock. Something's buried here."

Linc and Rosa dropped to their knees beside her. Fossils were sometimes uncovered in the area, as were artifacts left behind by the first peoples to inhabit the canyon. If that was the case, construction would stop until the area could be properly assessed and excavated.

That was time Angie didn't have.

But as Linc helped brush away the soil, it became evident what was buried was neither natural nor ancient. The side of a five-gallon plastic bucket emerged from the dirt. There was a cap on the top, sealed around the edges with a rubbery adhesive, likely designed to keep water out…

Or to keep whatever the bucket contained in.

Linc rocked on his heels and motioned for Rosa and Angie to back away.

Angie mimicked his posture. "What's wrong?"

He shook his head, thinking. It was possible the bucket had been discarded on the ranch some time ago. It was evident the thing had been in the ground for a while. But given how deep it was buried, it hadn't been covered naturally.

No, it had been purposely buried. Sealed, then buried. Almost like a time capsule.

He frowned. "Did you and Jacob ever bury a time capsule you planned to come back for in fifty years?" It was a long shot, but one he had to take.

Angie shook her head slowly. "No. Why?" She stiffened, her expression growing tense. "This is bad, isn't it?"

"I don't know." He pulled his phone from his pocket and dialed Thomas. Normally, he'd dig up the thing himself, but given that it was sealed, it could contain anything from hazardous waste to parts of human remains. He'd hate to disturb a crime scene.

What was the probability they'd find evidence of yet another crime on Angie's property?

Given the way things were going, the probability was astronomical. His gut said Angie's land was about to be the center of something much worse than they'd already imagined.

ELEVEN

The crime-scene unit had put a temporary open-sided tent over the area around the bucket and had set up spotlights to combat the coming nightfall. Linc and Thomas waited by a folding table for Erin Navarro to finish unearthing the bucket.

He'd sent Rosa and Angie to Rosa's cabin with Patricia Cassidy, the junior member of their team. While this could be an innocent discarded bucket, his gut said it was more. The seal led him to believe either someone had dumped industrial waste, or buried crucial evidence. "What's the likelihood this closes at least one of the cold cases we've had on the books for years?"

Thomas exhaled and crossed his arms over his chest, watching the crime-scene techs work. "The way you've told me things have been going out here the past couple of days, I'd say really good." He chewed his lower lip, studying the scene. "We may break several cases all at once if we can link ones we've been investigating to what's happening here."

He really didn't want to think about that until he needed to. "So you guys have been busy while I've been gone."

"No doubt." Dropping his arms, Thomas shoved his hands into his pockets. "We're waiting on cause of death for the hiker, though based on location and initial investigation, it looks like she fell. As always, we want to rule out homicide, though." Identification and a cell phone found on the remains the team had investigated earlier had named the woman as a missing hiker who was unaffiliated with the serial-killer case.

"At least you can rule out the serial killer."

"True. But we've still got two missing women."

"Isla Blake and…?" In the hubbub the day before, he'd never gotten a name for the second potential victim.

"Monica Huerta."

Linc's head came up. Why was that name familiar?

Thomas arched an eyebrow. "You know her?"

"No, but…" *Monica Huerta.* He'd heard it recently. He tried to cycle through the conversations he'd had over the past few days. So many names, places, faces… A lot had happened since Jacob had asked him to check on Angie a couple of nights earlier. Too many facts were flopping around his head like clothes in a dryer. Exhaustion, coupled with stress about his unanswered medical questions, made everything worse. When he got to the house, he'd flip through his notes and see if he'd written anything down. Could be it was one of the protestors who'd—

A flash of conversation. *Monica Huerta and I went to school together and now we go to church together, but we're more acquaintances than friends.*

"Monica Huerta is one of the protestors. Angie knows her."

Thomas turned toward Linc. "Wait. Not only is she missing in a way eerily similar to Isla Blake and seven women from a decade ago, but she's linked to the protests? And she's friends with Angie?"

"More of an acquaintance, I think, but yes." The web was tangling more than ever.

"Do you know when Angie last spoke to her?"

"I think she said it was before she went to Vegas, maybe two weeks ago? Monica reassured her they'd figured out who'd vandalized the ranch and had dealt with the problem, had turned the names over to the sheriff." He tried to remember more. "I think she might have said Monica was one of the organizers, but I'm not sure."

"I need to talk to Angie." Thomas's voice was grim.

Linc's heart sank with his teammate's tone. Interviewing Angie about Monica would pile onto an already heavy load. It would tell Angie someone she knew might be in danger. It might even drive home the truth a serial killer seemed to be hunting in the area.

He prayed not.

"If the serial killer is back, he's not after Angie." Thomas was studying Linc as though he could read his thoughts. "This guy approaches women online first, then somehow controls them enough to get them to hand over as much cash as they can easily access, along with enough info for him to steal their identities as well."

"Which is odd." Most of the women didn't have a lot of money, and what they got from ATM withdrawals didn't amount to much. It also risked putting them on camera, although that could be his way of taunting the authorities.

What made less sense was the identification. Why go to the trouble of forcing women to hand over their documents? "Unless he's got a lucrative side business going on, selling birth certificates and such on the black market."

"Risky business, giving someone the name of a dead woman, though."

"True." Thomas nodded toward the small group in protective gear as they cleared the bucket. "Frankly, all of this is convoluted and confusing. It's like Fairweather Ranch is suddenly the hub of criminal activity for the canyon."

Angie's attacks, the missing women, Ellis West's death… They all could be linked.

He stared at the group working around the bucket, and they seemed to be wrapping up. "Looks like we're about to take over here." And none too soon. This conversation was getting too personal.

Sure enough, Erin Navarro approached with the bucket and set it on the table between Linc and Thomas. "It's clear. No remains. No chemicals." She shrugged, her expression unreadable. "I'll take photos and document while you guys check it out."

Evidence discovery always kicked Linc's heart up a notch, but this time it felt as though his pulse might rocket to the stars beginning to twinkle in the night sky. Whatever was in the innocuous white five-gallon bucket was going to affect Angie—he had no doubt.

He hoped it wouldn't wreck her.

He tugged on gloves.

Thomas did the same, then motioned for Linc to do the honors.

With Erin documenting every step of the process, Linc removed the loosened lid and peered inside, leaving room for Thomas to look as well.

An oversize plastic zip-top bag rested in the bucket with a large brown mailing envelope sealed inside. Whatever it contained was thin. Duct tape further sealed the package. The person who had put it there clearly wanted to protect it from the elements.

Thomas watched closely as Lincoln slid the bag onto the table for Erin to photograph. "Think we're dealing with a treasure map?"

Lincoln actually chuckled. It would be a relief to discover someone had concocted a wild-goose chase for fake treasure rather than the host of more sinister things that could be at play.

Erin smiled. "Dibs on the map. We can keep a secret, right?"

"Sure." Thomas curled his lip. "You do realize every single bit of anything hypothetically hidden out there would go to the government. No 'finders keepers' for us."

"Yeah. Big sigh. Wreck my wild wishes with your boring truth." Erin snapped another photo. "My dad has a ton of those buckets in his garage from when he redid the bathroom when I was in high school. That was twelve years ago, so that bucket's probably not very old."

Twelve years. Linc glanced at Thomas. While the likelihood of this being linked to a serial killer from ten years earlier was slim, it felt too coincidental given everything else happening at the ranch.

"Let's see what we've got." Linc carefully cut away the duct tape, and Thomas bagged it. It was possible the conditions in the bucket had preserved fingerprints. He slid out the envelope and opened it, then tipped it to slide the contents onto the table.

A birth certificate. A social-security card. A passport. Several bank statements. And...

Linc picked up the paper and scanned it. A DD 214, a copy of a service record when someone separated from the military. He scanned the name on the top and passed it to Thomas.

His teammate grimly read the paper. "Janis Nichols." Dropping the document in line with the others, he stared at the row of horrifying evidence.

There was no reason for any of them to speak. The minute they'd seen the documents, they'd all known.

He couldn't look away from the table, couldn't stop himself from noting the only form of identification missing was the driver's license, which had been mailed to Janis Nichols's family ten years earlier, covered in her blood.

Thomas looked grim. "Well, we know our bad guy's not selling the identities. It looks like he's keeping trophies."

"I don't know." Erin eyed the documents spread out on the table. "Don't killers usually keep their trophies close or easily accessible? Why bury them in the middle of the Garcias' ranch?"

"Because he or she had a connection to the place." This was

the exact thing Lincoln had hoped wouldn't happen. Angie didn't need more trouble. Ellis's death had already—

"Wait. Erin's right." Killers liked to keep their prizes where they could see them, touch them, bring back the thrill of the kill. "These aren't trophies. These are preserved." Lines were drawing in Lincoln's mind, connecting ideas that had been random thoughts before. "Whoever buried these was keeping them safe."

"But why?" Thomas didn't look convinced. "To sell later?"

"I've got a wild thought." Really wild. First, he needed to confirm something. "Erin, you took photos of the West cabin. There was mail on his counter. Do you still have those on your camera?"

"Sure do." She started clicking as she watched the screen. "I uploaded them to our database, but I haven't wiped the memory card yet. What are you looking for?"

"A postcard." Something was tweaking his memory. "Thomas, the women went missing over a decade ago, right? And then it all stopped?"

"Yeah."

"Before or after Ellis West's father was killed in a car accident?"

Thomas tapped on his phone as Erin passed her camera across the table to Linc.

Linc studied the photo of the postcard. The front showed a glorious sunrise over the canyon. He clicked to the next image. Ellis's address was on one side along with a postmark from Houston two days before Ellis died. There was no return address or message, just a heart and the name *Nica*. He stared at the signature. "It would be odd to send a postcard of the canyon to someone who lived at the canyon, right?"

"A little," Erin said.

Thomas nodded. "Not out of the realm of possibility, but odd. And the disappearances ended about five weeks before

Javi West and Angie's father died." He looked up, pocketing his phone. "What are you thinking, Tucker?"

"That there's never been a single body found for any of these missing women. The only evidence that they were killed or injured is their blood on their IDs." He looked up at Erin. "I want someone to go through Ellis's things and see if there's another postcard similar to this one. I also want to know of any reports of domestic violence around any of the missing women." He held up the camera so Thomas could see and maybe follow along with his train of thought. "Nica could be short for—"

"Monica." Thomas's eyes widened as he caught on. "That would be… You think…?"

"I *suspect*," Linc clarified as he handed the camera back to Erin. "What if the identification and money were taken as insurance? And buried out here for safekeeping? What if Ellis West's father and possibly Angie's father were helping these women escape something? And what if Ellis was following in his father's footsteps?"

"And what if that postcard was a way to communicate a safe arrival in a new location?" Thomas already had his phone out again. "I'm getting on those records now. Because if you're right…"

If he was right, those women were still alive and hiding from something horrible.

Without concrete evidence, they still had to investigate as though the women had been kidnapped and murdered, but this was definitely a trail to follow, and it might provide a motive for Ellis West's murder.

Because the best way to save someone's life was to make it look like they were already dead.

"Wait." Angie sank onto the couch that sat squarely in front of the stone fireplace in Rosa's living room. The way the space had seemed to tilt when Linc's teammate Thomas spoke, she didn't trust herself to remain standing. "Repeat that. Please." *But say something totally different than what I heard the first time.*

Sending a pointed look toward Thomas, Lincoln sat beside her and faced her, resting a hand on her knee. "Where do you need me to start?"

Forget starting. She wanted this to be finished. No more surprises.

But that was impossible unless this was a nightmare.

It wasn't. The last time she'd checked, she'd definitely been awake.

Might as well begin with the worst. "So Carter was right and there really is a serial killer?"

Linc stared at her for a long time before he finally spoke. "We've found evidence that might link some women who disappeared in the past to two women who disappeared recently." Linc's voice was low and gentle, as though he was trying to calm a skittish horse.

That creeped her out way more than if he'd spoken in normal tones. "Talk to me like I'm me, Linc, not like I'm a kindergartner who doesn't understand math."

His teeth dug into his lower lip. Surely he wasn't biting back a smile at a time like this? "That bucket contained identification documents belonging to a woman who vanished a decade ago when several women were taken by someone the federal authorities believe was a serial killer."

"Are they trophies?" Her voice pitched to an octave that might have shattered eardrums. "You found a serial killer's trophies on my property?"

"Angie, I—"

She threw up a hand, nearly smacking Linc in the face. *No.* More words weren't going to fix this. "I need a second." Her thoughts spun. Ten years ago, someone had murdered women. Someone who'd likely been connected to the ranch. Sure, back then the property had been in its last years as a dude ranch, so anyone could have buried that bucket. But to place it so close to the main cabins?

Her stomach dipped and twisted. No one would dare to hide something in that spot unless they had unfettered access. "A decade ago, a killer probably lived on my family's ranch." She had been away at school. So had Jacob, but there had been ranch hands, visitors… Pressing her fingers to her lips, she looked across the room at Rosa, whose expression was as stricken as her own had to be. While Rosa hadn't worked for the ranch then, this was too close to home for both of them.

Rosa drew in a shuddering breath. "I'll get you the employee records from then." Her words were soft, almost resigned. The idea anyone connected with Fairweather could do such a thing was horrifying.

One more horror to add to a growing list. If only she could roll back the clock to Sunday night, when her biggest problem had been losing a grant to Owen. She'd thought that was the worst that could happen.

It certainly paled in comparison to everything that had occurred since. Attacks. Murder. Serial killers. "What next, Linc? When does this end?" *Are there bodies buried on my land?*

She couldn't bring herself to ask. The answer might be more than she could handle.

She'd sure picked the wrong day to start feeling her emotions.

"I hope it ends soon." Linc squeezed her hand and released it.

She studied his face, and he didn't look away.

He was leaving something out. As much as she wanted to demand to know more, rationality said she was better off letting Linc decide what might be too much for her to handle. After all, she'd passed being overwhelmed hours ago.

From where he stood near the fireplace, Thomas spoke. "We

don't think you've been targeted by a serial killer." Thomas was tall and thin, more bull rider than federal investigator. His dark hair was short, and though she knew he and Linc were both in their early thirties, salt had already streaked through the brown. Unlike Linc, he wasn't a fidgeter. He stood extraordinarily still, as though disturbing the air in the room might upset some delicate balance. Despite his rigid stance, his brown eyes were compassionate. "I wish we had more answers."

So did she.

Linc withdrew his hand from her knee and pivoted so he sat straight on the couch, no longer facing her. Instead, he stared at the coffee table, which was strewn with files and papers. Contracts were scattered over the top of the mess, and a yellow legal pad filled with numbers sat in the middle of it all. Rosa had been working through their financial mess, trying to figure out how to cover costs with the grant gone and their current group of scientists off-site due to the investigation.

Angie stared at her fingers, clasped between her knees. Her brain didn't want to consider all of the options in front of her. Or, more realistically, the *lack* of options in front of her.

"We also don't think the protestors have been directly involved in the attacks on you the past few days, outside of the one at the hospital. Given what Riley has said, the working theory is that whoever paid them is behind that." With a heavy sigh, Thomas sat on the other side of the coffee table and leaned forward, mimicking her posture with his hands clasped between his knees. "We do have some questions about the protestors, though."

"Okay." But if the protestors weren't directly involved, why did it matter?

"You told Linc you knew one of the local organizers."

"Sort of. We went to school together. We attend the same church, but we have a large congregation so we don't cross paths a lot."

Thomas jotted something in a notebook he pulled from his pocket. Like Linc, he seemed to prefer pen and paper. "What's her name?"

"Monica Huerta." Surely they didn't think… "Monica wouldn't hurt me. She's always been friendly. She even apologized for any trouble the protestors caused. She's the one who told me they'd turned over the vandals to the sheriff."

Looking up, Thomas studied her with one eyebrow raised. "Why would she help organize a protest if she's sorry for doing it?"

"You'd have to ask her to be sure, but Monica has ancestral ties to the Havasupai. She's proud of her heritage. If she somehow came to believe, like the protestors seem to, that I was going to hurt the land, then I can understand her being upset. The fact it's me, someone she knows, wouldn't change her convictions. I just wish she'd talk to me about what I'm truly doing. She might understand I want to help preserve history and heritage by providing a place for research and preservation. I want to be part of the solution."

Again, Thomas wrote in his notebook. He flipped a few pages and read something.

The silence grew long. Even Rosa, who was normally steady, shifted as though she couldn't get comfortable. She fired a grim look at Angie.

Lincoln stood and walked to the window, looking out as though he felt caged.

She could appreciate that. Every ounce of her longed for a wild run on her horse, but not to the canyon. Now she wanted to ride headlong deep into the forest, where she wouldn't feel so exposed.

"When did you last speak to Monica?" Thomas didn't look up.

"At church a couple of weeks ago. That's when she told me about the sheriff." There were too many questions about

Monica. This had to be what Linc wasn't talking about. Angie stood and faced him. "Linc, what are you hiding? Did Monica do something?"

When Linc turned from the window, it was to carry on a silent conversation with Thomas. The look they exchanged spoke of a discussion already completed, a plan already in place.

When Linc walked closer, Angie backed away. "What?" There was a wild extra beat to her heart. The news wasn't going to be good.

"Monica's missing." Linc's voice was quiet but firm, leaving no room for her to argue with the facts.

"That's impossible." She'd argue whether he liked it or not. "I saw her before I went to the conference."

The room was heavy with silence that crashed her protests to the hardwood. No one would look at her. Even Rosa stared at the fireplace, seeming stricken by paralysis.

"Do they think...?" If they were talking about serial killers, then they thought Monica was a victim.

"I'm sorry." Thomas closed his notebook, keeping his finger tucked into the spot where he'd been writing. "I know this is a lot, but can you tell me about your last conversation? Remember anything else she might have said? Anything unusual about her behavior?"

Thoughts swirled. There was too much information assaulting her. She closed her eyes and tried to picture the large sanctuary and how Monica had looked.

Nothing stood out. It had been a brief conversation, and Monica had simply squeezed her shoulder in a quick side hug before she left. "I'm sorry. I've got nothing."

"She hasn't mentioned talking to anyone online?"

"We weren't close enough to talk like that." If only she could remember more. "It was a quick conversation. She was on her way to get her sister from children's church."

Linc leaned forward. "How old is her sister?"

"Sasha is much younger. I think seven or eight?"

Linc turned to Thomas. "Has anyone from our team interviewed the family yet?"

"No." Thomas slipped his notebook into the leg pocket of his uniform. "I'm supposed to do that tomorrow morning."

"I'll go." Linc looked down at Angie. "We'll both go."

Thomas moved as though he was going to say more, but he seemed to think better of it and simply nodded. "Call me when you're done."

Angie stared at Linc. He was up to something. She had no idea what, but she was along for the ride, whether she liked it or not.

TWELVE

Lincoln locked the dead bolt and punched the alarm code Angie had given him to arm the system. By the time he turned around, Angie was halfway up the stairs, her shoulders slumped as though the weight on her shoulders was more than she could bear.

It most assuredly was.

The last thing Angie needed was to be alone. She might think she needed quiet, but he'd been around long enough to know how deep she could dive into her own head. With all she had going on, she needed to talk it out, maybe get a notebook and write it out, but she certainly didn't need to let everything simply sit.

He'd taken one step toward the stairs and was about to call her name when his phone buzzed. A glance at the notification on his watch told him he dare not ignore this one.

It was his doctor's office, likely calling to confirm his appointment.

He winced. If he went to interview Monica Huerta's family in the morning, he would have to push back receiving his results.

Again.

He pressed the answer button and held the phone to his ear, waiting for the recording to tell him which number to push to reschedule.

Instead, there was silence.

His forehead creased. "This is Lincoln Tucker."

"Special Agent Tucker." The voice was familiar. "It's Dr. Collins."

His doctor. She wasn't waiting until morning to tell him the results to his face.

Suddenly his knees didn't want to hold him. The next few seconds would determine the course of his future. He would continue to live the life he loved, or he would lose everything.

He sank to the arm of the sofa. Shifting the phone to his other ear, he cleared his throat as emotion tried to clog it. "Can I return to full duty?" Why bother with formalities? He knew why she was calling. She knew what he wanted to hear.

She was the kind of no-nonsense doc who understood. She'd been a surgeon in the army and now worked with veterans and the National Park Service. She understood the language. Pass on the news, get in and get out, keep moving at all costs.

"I know from speaking to the clinic's receptionist you're working a case, so I thought I'd call rather than have you pulled out of the field to come in." The words were kind, but they were also brusque.

The tone…

Lincoln had never felt his heart sink before, but he was pretty sure it landed somewhere around his feet.

She didn't need to say more.

His eyes slipped shut. His entire body tensed, pushing a deep ache from his spine into his head. He'd known all along. No matter how much he'd tried to fool himself, the pain always told him otherwise.

Silence reigned for several heartbeats, then the doc exhaled. "I'm sorry, Agent Tucker. I even got a second and a third opinion before I called you, and you have access to your scans so you can get a fourth, but given the current state of your injury and the rate at which it's healing, I can't clear you to return to full duty."

"Now or ever?" Man, he hated the way the words cracked.

"I didn't necessarily say that. We'll revisit this in a few months, but…"

His arm threatened to go limp, but he pressed the phone tighter to his ear. "Surgery is still out of the question?"

"Too risky, as we've discussed in the past. The chances of permanent paralysis are high. Once you go through physical therapy and this initial pain subsides, you'll be free to live a normal life, but you'll have to curb some of your riskier activities, to include climbing and rappelling." She hesitated. "I know this is a lot, and I'm sorry to tell you over the phone. Schedule an appointment when you're done with your current case, and we'll go over your options, okay?" Her voice softened, clearly affected by his pain. "This may not be forever."

Well, he didn't want the pity. "Yeah." He killed the call without saying goodbye then stared at the phone, clenched in his white-knuckle grip. What he wanted was to throw it across the room and watch it smash against the wall. It took everything he had to behave like an adult.

No climbing. No rappelling. That likely meant no backcountry hiking, possibly no horseback riding. The doc might as well lock him in a closet. Bury pieces of him in that bucket they'd unearthed. If he couldn't do those things, he was useless to his team.

Nothing else mattered.

"Hey." A touch on his shoulder nearly sent him through the ceiling.

He whirled toward the voice.

Angie withdrew her hand but didn't back away, the way he would have in her position. Instead, she studied him with concern. "That call didn't sound good."

He stared down at her, trying to pull his mind into reality. He'd forgotten where he was and that she was in the house. The way his brain spun, her presence wasn't computing, and for the quickest moment, he couldn't separate past from present.

With one brief shake of his head, he paced to the breakfast bar between the kitchen and the living area, then to the dining-room table. He couldn't force himself to stand still. His future had disintegrated while his past stood in front of him.

He wanted to run.

There was nowhere to go.

Had it only been a few hours since he'd watched Angie pace this same route around the living room, frustrated and fright-ened? Now here he was, wearing the same groove in the floor.

He stopped in front of a large china cabinet filled with knickknacks her mother had left behind when she moved in with her sister. Photos, seashells and art were nestled behind the glass doors.

His own mother had never been one to keep "treasures."

How was he going to explain to his family the job he'd com-mitted his life to was gone? They'd have plenty to say. He'd failed and had nothing to show for—

Angie's hand rested at the center of his back, below the damaged place in his spine, warm and... And tender. "I'm sorry."

"You didn't do anything." Somehow the words came out at half volume. In the glass front of the cabinet, he could make out the shape of her reflection.

She was watching him in the glass. "I know how much your job means to you. I know you wanted a different answer. I know right now everything feels broken."

His chin dropped to his chest, tugging at the pain. At this moment, he didn't want anyone to understand. He wanted to be angry and hurt. To punch a wall or run until his legs gave out. He didn't want sympathy.

Yet, he couldn't move away from her touch.

Silently, Angie turned and rested her forehead on his shoulder. It wasn't a gesture that spoke of pity. It was a gesture that offered strength.

She didn't feel sorry for him. She wanted to help him stand against the winds of this storm.

After their friendship died, he'd never expected to partner with her in anything again. Had never imagined the two of them could be there for one another in trying times.

Yet here they were. He was walking her through a nightmare. She was supporting him in a hurricane.

How was that kind of grace possible?

Soft warmth flowed from his brain to his heart, then rushed out to his fingertips.

This was right. This was what the two of them were meant to be, what he'd slaughtered with his awkward self-centeredness years before.

She needed him, and he needed her. There had been a gaping hole inside of him ever since he'd walked out the door that day. He'd missed her laugh and her smile, her honesty and her vulnerability. Most of all, he'd missed her friendship. Her presence.

With an exhale he'd been holding for years, he slid his arm around her waist and gently pulled her against his chest. Resting his chin on the top of her head, he simply held on.

Her back stiffened. For a moment, she didn't breathe, and he thought she might pull away. Then her arms slipped around his waist and she pressed her cheek against his chest. She was bound to be able to hear the effect she had on his heart rate.

She didn't let go. She simply held on as though she could keep him from flying apart.

Maybe she could. Or, better yet, maybe God could, through her. The one thing he'd learned over the years was God mattered most. Somehow, God had given him the gift of Angie's presence to help him through.

Even more, God had given him the gift of helping Angie

through. He wasn't useless. Pointless. Helpless. She needed him, and he was available because of the careless mistake that might have cost him his career.

The anger faded, though he knew it would return to fight another day. In this moment, his shattered dreams weren't as important as protecting Angie.

He was where he needed to be.

His head dipped, and his cheek brushed hers. Her breath was warm against his ear, and it hitched in a way that said she felt the same rush that ran through him. Warm emotion flowed through his veins, bringing the vision of a new future, a dream he'd only considered one other time. A dream he'd kept under lock and key.

One that now saw daylight as his former dreams fell to pieces.

If Angie turned her head…

If he turned his…

This moment could go very differently. He could pour into her everything he was feeling. This gratitude. This new awareness of what she meant to him. He could say it all without words. Could promise her something new, something neither of them had ever dared to hope for.

Her head tipped ever so slightly.

Lincoln backed away, wanting to see her expression, to measure her emotions. He let his gaze roam her eyes, her face, her lips. With his entire being, he wanted to close the gap and pour everything into a kiss that would change their worlds all over again.

But he couldn't.

It took all of the strength he held in reserve to back away from her, to let his hands fall to his sides and to deny himself what he wanted most.

Because kissing her here, now, when they were both emotionally exhausted and pushed to their mental limits, would be too much like the last time he'd kissed her, when they'd nearly thrown everything over a cliff's edge.

He couldn't layer that moment over this one. Couldn't let their past mistakes color a precious heartbeat that might lead to a different future.

No, he wanted to start at the beginning. To treat her with the care and tenderness she deserved.

Cupping her cheeks in his palms, he pressed a kiss to her forehead. Then he pulled her into a hug he hoped would convey all of the things he couldn't say.

What was happening to her life?

Angie pulled the seat belt from her chest and let it thread through her fingers as it slipped into place. Through the plate glass window of Misty's eclectic gas station/gift shop/lunch counter, Linc kept one eye on Angie in the truck and one eye on the conversation he was having with Misty, who nodded before she disappeared through a door in the back of the store.

Angie eyed the gravel parking lot, empty in the gap between breakfast and lunch. Linc had insisted they stop on the way to talk to Monica's family, giving her no explanation for this detour.

Just like he hadn't given her an explanation for his behavior the night before.

She leaned her head against the window and stared at him, unsure if he could see her through the sunlight reflecting off the truck's windshield. Their silent conversation had touched something deep inside her, unraveling years of pain that had formed the night her grief had pushed him one step too far.

The memory heated her cheeks, the shame still stinging.

Somehow, last night had provided a salve that made the burn less raw.

When she'd walked down the stairs and heard Lincoln's clipped phone conversation, she'd sensed his loss as clearly as if he'd broadcast the words with a skywriter. The doctor's news had thrown his future off a ledge. He'd been seconds from dashing his hopes on the rocks at the bottom.

His slumped shoulders, pained expression and white-knuckle grip on his phone had made her pain fade. Letting him know he was seen had become the most important thing.

No words would have done that, so she'd held him and let him hold her.

And in the process...

Well, in the process everything had changed.

She could still feel the way he'd clung to her. For a moment she'd nearly bolted, horrified by the fact that she'd drawn them into that space where they'd nearly made an irreversible misstep years ago.

This time was different.

This time, that broken wounded mess they'd both been had somehow knit itself together. It wasn't about feeling alive or hiding from the horror of a brother's brokenness and pain.

This time, it had been about sharing one another's hurts. Understanding one another's feelings. The last time they'd approached each other, it had been all about her, about escaping the emotion and exhaustion.

This time, all she'd wanted was to help him hold it together. To let him know he wasn't alone.

The change inside of her was monumental. The shift in her thinking and the crack straight down the middle of her heart indicated she was no longer the same person.

She'd accepted God's forgiveness long ago, but the barrier between Linc and herself had seemed insurmountable. That had all changed when Linc pressed a kiss to her forehead, then held her as though she was fragile, although he was, too.

In that moment, she forgave him.

In that moment, she forgave herself.

Now, sitting in Linc's truck, still fearing for her safety, her heart was raw and the tears were close. Her past mistakes no longer defined her, not with Linc and not with anyone else. For the first time, she truly understood what it meant to be made new.

As Linc walked out the door of Misty's carrying a huge box, she studied him. While she knew this shift had changed her relationship with Jesus, had made it more real and much deeper, she had no idea what it meant for her relationship with Linc.

Was there a future?

Did she want one?

He stashed the box in the bed of his pickup, then slid behind the wheel without looking at her. He'd been quiet all morning. Given the news he'd received, he was probably wrestling with reality.

She let a few miles go by, trying not to think about everything happening in and around her. It would probably be easier on them both if she could start a conversation, but the silence felt too heavy.

So heavy she had to break it. "It's going to storm later." The pressure was dropping, and although it was only mid-morning, cumulonimbus clouds were already building. It was a volatile time of year around the canyon. Hopefully, they'd avoid flooding rains.

"Really? We're going to talk about the weather?" It was tough to tell if that was sarcasm or amusement in his voice.

She opted to believe it was amusement and pushed toward something slightly more personal. "What's in the box?"

He kept his eyes on the road as they approached the outskirts of Williams. "You said Monica has a younger sister."

"Sasha. She's not in that box, though."

He arched an eyebrow, an indication her attempt at humor had fallen flat. "No, but with her sister missing, there's a lot of turmoil around her. I figured with the variety of stuff Misty sells, I might find something to help the kid out." He slowed and made a turn onto a narrow street, studying house numbers.

The homes here were small and packed tightly together. It was a neighborhood in transition, an eclectic mix of aging original and newly remodeled, of well-kept lawns and overgrown yards.

He parked in front of a small house with a brick facade and an older sedan in the driveway. Large windows dominated the front of the structure, though the curtains were drawn.

Linc looked at her for the first time since he'd returned to the vehicle. "I'm going to talk with Monica's parents and likely ask some hard questions. You're here to make me less intimidating."

Under normal circumstances, that blunt declaration would have made her laugh. The truth removed all humor from the situation. "I'm here because you didn't want to leave me at the ranch."

"That, too. Look, I—" Linc shook his head, as though gnats were buzzing around him, then abruptly shoved the door open. "I need to focus on this right now." He left the truck and slammed the door behind him.

Okay, then. Angie slipped out of the vehicle and followed Linc and his mysterious box to the front door.

It opened before they reached it, and a middle-aged man stepped out. He was shorter than Linc and thin, his skin darkened and lined by the sun. "Can I help you?" Wary exhaustion weighted the words.

Linc set the box on the low brick porch wall and lifted his badge where it hung on a chain around his neck. "I'm Special Agent Lincoln Tucker with the National Park Service Investigative Services. We're helping to search for Monica. I spoke to her mother earlier."

The man's posture relaxed and he stepped aside, holding the door open. "I'm her father, Martin. Her mother's inside."

Linc let Angie walk in ahead of him, and she stepped from bright midmorning sunlight into oppressive darkness. The curtains were closed. The lights were off. The air felt heavy and still. As her eyes adjusted, she took in a crowded living room stuffed with mismatched furniture. A counter with overhanging cabinets separated the living area from the kitchen.

A familiar woman about Angie's height walked out of the kitchen carrying a coffee cup. At her heels was Monica's sister, Sasha, carefully pulling the paper from a muffin.

Mrs. Huerta stopped abruptly when she saw Angie. "Oh. I'm sorry." She looked past Angie to Linc. "I forgot you were coming." Her head tilted as she returned her gaze to Angie. "You go to church with us."

How did someone forget that law enforcement was coming to help search for their missing daughter? It took a second to comprehend the second part of Mrs. Huerta's statement. "Oh. Monica and I went to school together, and yes, I go to Daybridge with you, Mrs. Huerta."

"Call me Celia."

"Celia. I'm so sorry about—"

"Sit. Please." Mrs. Huerta motioned to the couch near the front window as Mr. Huerta shut the door and sat in a recliner. "Coffee?"

"I'm fine." Everything felt odd, stilted. Maybe that was normal. She'd never been around a family whose daughter might have been taken by a serial killer, so who was she to judge their behavior?

As Angie sat, Linc settled the box in the middle of the floor. "I brought something for Sasha. Is that okay?"

The little girl peered from behind her mother, then looked up for permission to approach.

Mrs. Huerta nodded.

Sasha shoved the muffin into her mother's hand and lunged for the box. She ripped open the flaps then dove inside to retrieve the contents.

Angie bit back a laugh as Sasha squealed in delight at the

massive stuffed animal. Taller than the little girl, the unicorn was a riot of pastel colors and featured a squishy gold lamé horn. Sasha dove on top of the toy and sprawled like it was a bed, her smile radiant. "Thank you!"

Linc offered a smile as he kneeled beside her. He tapped the gold horn. "I figured now would be a good time for a new best friend."

Sasha threw her arms around the plush unicorn's neck and held on tight. "I love it!" As fast as only a small child could move, she leaped at Linc and wrapped her arms around his neck. "Thank you, Mr. Policeman. I love you, too."

Linc winced, then his eyes closed and he hugged the little girl tight before she squirmed away and turned to her mother. "Can I take it to my room?"

"Sure."

Sasha hugged Linc again, admiration and maybe the beginnings of a little-girl crush in her expression. He'd brought joy into her rocky world, had considered her feelings when she'd probably been shoved to the side by circumstances.

Angie looked away, her heart squeezing in her chest with feelings she was only beginning to acknowledge.

I can relate, Sasha. I can relate.

THIRTEEN

Some moments reminded him there was still good in the world.

Linc was reluctant to let this one go.

Sasha shouted another thank-you and dragged her prize down the narrow hallway out of sight, taking some of the sparkle from the room and reminding him why he was really here. Not to brighten the day of a little girl whose world had been turned upside down, but to talk to the parents of a woman who had vanished, either on her own or at the hands of a serial killer.

He rose, trying not to wince at the pain being tackled by a seven-year-old had inflicted. Glancing around the room, he chose a seat in a side chair instead of taking a spot on the couch by Angie.

Being near her messed with his senses. The entire ride to Williams, he'd been distracted by her instead of working through the questions he needed to ask the Huertas. She'd unlocked something in him the previous evening, and he had no idea what to do with it. This was different than the last time they'd walked through trials together. There was no desperate sense of need. This was quiet. Deeper. It bordered on lo—

He drew a deep breath. He needed to focus, not only to help locate Monica Huerta, but also to uncover any clues that might point to who had killed Ellis and attacked Angie.

From where she stood by the kitchen entrance, Mrs. Huerta

offered a tight smile. "Thank you, Agent Tucker. She's been a bit out of sorts with everything that's happened. Since Monica has been living on her own for a while now, Sasha hasn't processed the day-to-day of Monica's being gone, but she has certainly picked up on our tension. That present was a bright spot for her." She walked over and sat on the opposite end of the couch from Angie. "Are you sure I can't offer you anything?"

"I'm fine. Thank you." He pulled his notebook from his thigh pocket and glanced around the room, trying to appear casual.

In his peripherals, he watched the Huertas. Martin sat rigid, his gaze on his wife as though she was in control of what happened next.

Celia held her coffee cup lightly, seeming to be calm. It was clearly an act. Her posture was stiff, and her words were measured and carefully chosen. While people for whom English was a second language often spoke formally due to their lack of idioms or contractions, he knew from reading the case notes that Celia had been raised in an English-speaking home.

Something else was going on. There was a practiced air to her movements. He'd seen families react oddly under stress, but this?

The vibe was off in the Huerta household, and it made him wonder if the theory he'd shared with Thomas actually held water.

He stared at a blank page in his notebook, pretending to study words that weren't there. He'd have to be careful how he presented himself, or they'd shut him out.

When he finally looked up, Martin was still watching his wife, and Celia sat with her coffee mug resting on her bent knees, her straight posture and crossed ankles reminding him of photos of the British royal family.

The most truthful answers would likely come from the father. He angled toward Martin. "Sir, I know this is difficult.

You've answered a thousand questions for the local police, but my team is working with the FBI and I have some follow-up questions." He guarded his words, not wanting to guide the Huertas' answers.

"I don't understand why the FBI is involved." Martin stared at work-worn hands, balling his fists as though he was holding in emotion. Fear? Anger? Whatever it was, it was volatile. His body language betrayed his calm words.

"It's standard when someone disappears under these sorts of circumstances. You're going to hear me repeat a lot of questions, so I apologize in advance."

Martin's gaze flicked to his wife, a hard look that seemed like a challenge. He worked his mouth from side to side, then met Linc's gaze with what was almost a look of defiance. "Whatever you need. I just want to know my daughter is safe." He shot a hard look to his wife before staring at the floor.

The nagging feeling that something was off grew stronger. "We'll do everything we can, sir." He ran down a few basic questions about the last time they'd seen Monica and whether they knew anything about the man she'd been chatting with online. Their answers were consistent with the intel Thomas had already given him. "Where did Monica work? It was after she failed to show up for a shift that you noticed something was wrong, correct?"

Celia nodded, turning her coffee cup in her hands. "Yes. Her boss called. She worked as a plumber's apprentice and missed several appointments she'd been assigned."

Angie leaned forward, her forehead creased. Clearly, that had surprised her.

Martin's head jerked up, his eyes wide, but he quickly looked away from his wife toward the hallway where his daughter had disappeared.

Everything about this was weird, including that answer. Angie and Thomas had both told him Monica worked as a manager at an apartment complex. "She was a plumber's apprentice?"

"Part-time." When Celia looked at him, the fire in her eyes was totally out of place given the circumstances. "She used to talk to the plumber who did work for the complex, and he told her she could make more money hands-on than she could behind a desk. So she worked in the mornings as his apprentice and at the apartments in the afternoon and evenings."

"Who was this plumber?" *Was the FBI aware of this?*

"A man named Mac."

Angie seemed to jump, almost as though the name had jerked her into the room from somewhere else. "Mac Dwyer?"

Martin stood suddenly.

Linc eyed him, ready to intervene if necessary. The man moved like a caged animal. "Is everything okay, Mr. Huerta?"

"We're done talking. If you need anything, I'm sure the FBI can provide it. My family has been through enough." Martin walked to the door and pulled it open. "If you'd like to come back in a few days, maybe we can arrange something."

He'd learn nothing more today. Nodding slowly, Linc rose and waited for Angie to join him. He flipped his notebook closed and shoved it in his pocket. "I understand. This is a trying time, and I'm sure it's difficult to keep repeating your story." He pulled a business card from his pocket and laid it on the arm of the couch. "If you need me or you think of something that might help us find your daughter—"

Find your daughter. Like a key in a lock, his nagging thoughts clicked into place. He knew what was wrong.

He glanced around the room, attempting to make eye contact, but neither parent looked his way. "Please, don't hesitate to call." Motioning to Angie, he walked out the door, holding himself together until he got into the truck and started the engine. He needed to call Thomas, ASAP.

Angie snapped her seat belt. "You learned something, didn't you?"

Staring at the closed front door, Linc shook his head then backed out of the driveway. The Huertas were probably watching. Once he was out of the neighborhood and onto State Route 64 heading north, he felt like he'd sorted through the details enough to speak. "Something's not right."

"Their daughter is missing. There's a lot that's not right."

"No." He kneaded the steering wheel, forming his words carefully. Things often stood out to him that others missed. It was part training, part instinct. But this? This had been obvious. How much should he reveal to Angie? "Did you notice how they talked about Monica's disappearance? 'We want to know our daughter is safe.' Stuff like that?"

"Seems natural to me."

"I've worked dozens of missing-persons cases. Parents, spouses…they all inevitably say 'find my daughter' or 'bring my child home.' They bargain. They beg. They'll do anything, offer anything. But the Huertas?"

Angie sank into her seat and stared out the front windshield. "None of that happened. It was all—"

"Controlled. Like they had something to hide." It was as though they were reading from a script. But who had written their lines?

He reined in his thoughts and tried to think through all of the angles, not just the ones that matched his theory. People reacted to trauma in different ways. It was best to gather evidence with an impartial eye, but he still wanted to run all of this by Thomas soon.

Besides, he had more questions. "How did you know the plumber's name?"

Angie hesitated. "He subcontracts with Carter and did all of the plumbing work when we built the dorm and the lab."

Linc turned to her, then had to jerk his attention to the two-lane road. "What?" There had definitely been some weirdness in the air when Mac's name came up. He was connected directly to Monica, and as a subcontractor, he was connected through Carter to Isla Blake.

Due to the construction, Mac also had access to Angie's property.

They might not have reached two plus two equals four yet, but they were getting close.

Angie gripped the edge of her seat. "Whatever you're thinking, no. Mac is… He's pushing seventy. He plays Santa at church every Christmas and buys gifts for kids who wouldn't get gifts otherwise. He's constantly giving money or food or clothing to people who need it. He's practically everybody's grandfather. Mac was good friends with my dad and with Javi West, Ellis's father. He even recommended… He…" She exhaled something that sounded like word salad.

When he pulled his eyes from the road, she was staring past him, her mouth slightly open. "Angie? What do you remember?"

"Ellis West used to work for Mac. We hired him as a ranch hand on Mac's recommendation."

Linc pressed the Bluetooth button on his steering wheel. He was calling Thomas right now. He wanted Mac Dwyer brought in and questioned immediately.

Either that man had helped those women disappear…or he was guilty of murder.

Angie had been right earlier. Another storm was rolling in.

As a gust whipped the tape around the excavation site, Linc stood beside Thomas and watched the crime-scene units from the FBI and the National Park Service stow tents before rising wind could rip them away.

Thomas looked grim. "They've been out here since daybreak, and they've found nothing." He shoved his hands into his pockets and watched the activity. "Maybe the other evidence either doesn't exist, or it's buried somewhere else."

Linc let his gaze sweep the surrounding area. Stands of trees dotted the landscape at the edge of the Kaibab National Forest. Nearer the canyon, very little marred the space between horizon and sky.

The Garcias owned over a thousand acres, nearly two square miles of land. Beyond their inholding, two miles of government-owned land ran to the canyon, which was nearly two thousand largely untouched square miles. The Garcias' land ran several hundred feet into the national forest, which contained over a million pristine acres. Each held secrets they'd kept for thousands of years. There was no way to dig up every square inch of the land. Even ground-penetrating radar wouldn't help. It would be like mowing millions of square acres and hoping for a hit.

He watched storm clouds roil over the canyon in the distance. "I don't know. It's all too coincidental not to mean something. Ellis is murdered after two women disappear for the first time in a decade. The original disappearances stopped when Ellis's father died. Mac Dwyer knew Monica and has a connection to Isla plus access to this place."

"Where Ellis and his father both lived."

"And then there's that postcard…" That was the one thing that seemed to tie everything together. The most crucial piece of evidence was often the one thing that didn't make sense. That postcard stood out like a scream in the silence.

Thomas shook his head. "This is as close as you're ever going to get to a literal needle in a haystack."

He was right. They could search for decades and never find another clue. It was like playing *Battleship* on an infinite grid. One inch to the left and they'd miss the prize entirely.

"And, Tucker? If you're right and those women faked their own deaths, then they ran away from something. A couple of them had domestic calls to their houses. One had escaped trafficking. They may not want us to find them."

That was likely true, but until they had proof the women weren't victims of a killer, they were obligated to keep searching. Lincoln swept his hands over his hair, trying to right what the wind had wronged. It was futile. "Any word on Mac Dwyer?" That's where the answers were. They'd been unable to locate him at work or at home and were waiting for search warrants before they could proceed.

"Nothing yet."

"So we still don't know anything?" Angie's voice was tense.

Linc turned.

As she approached, she swept her wind-whipped hair out of her face and held it against the top of her head. She frowned when she caught his eye. "Before you ask, I didn't recognize anything other than a couple of names from news stories when I was a kid."

She'd been with Rosa since they returned from Williams, poring over unclassified portions of the files about all of the missing women, attempting to see if anything rang a bell.

Because they were still technically searching for a serial killer until evidence proved otherwise, Rosa had handed over old employee records to Thomas, who'd passed them on to the team and the FBI. They had set up a remote office in the research facility and were busily cross-referencing with the missing women, searching for connections. So far, they'd come up short.

Thomas excused himself to take a call and walked around the corner of Ellis's cabin, probably to get out of the wind. The sun still shone overhead, but it made the clouds in the distance appear darker and more ominous.

It almost felt like a sign of things to come.

Angie stared at the incoming storm. "It's a volatile time of year. Aren't you worried about destroying evidence?"

"Whatever's out here has been here for years. Anything that could be destroyed is long gone." Linc kicked the dirt. There were places where the topsoil was too shallow to bury five-gallon buckets, so they could eliminate those areas, but that still left too much land to cover.

It was hopeless.

"Angie." Rosa walked out of her cabin, pocketing her phone as she hurried across the path. "I've got to go to my mother's."

Angie turned to her, hands outstretched. "What's wrong? Is she okay? Do you need me to come along?"

"No. She's…" Rosa's face was pinched. The lines around her mouth were white. "She's had another seizure and is refusing to go to the hospital. I may need to stay with her tonight."

"Go." Angie waved her hands toward Rosa's cabin. "We'll be fine here."

Hesitating, Rosa looked at the crime-scene tape that twisted in a frenzy with the rising wind. "I don't want to leave you alone."

"She's not alone." Linc stepped closer to the woman, who was clearly distraught. Given that her mother had refused medical treatment for seizures before, he could understand Rosa's concern.

The news about his own test results nagged. He never wanted to make someone feel responsible for him, nor did he want to saddle someone else with his pain.

His gaze went to Angie, then he turned toward where Thomas had disappeared.

He wanted more from her than friendship. The more he was with her, the more he wanted to be with her. He wanted to share life, good and bad.

He wanted forever.

The thrill ran through him so quickly, he half wondered if lightning had reached across the miles and hit him square in the spine. It sure felt like electricity. The ferocity of the emotion melded his feet to the ground.

He loved her.

He'd loved her since the moment she'd comforted him in that hospital waiting room years earlier. He'd walked away because he'd wanted what was best for her...

Because. He. Loved. Her.

Did he love her enough to walk away again, knowing his injury could leave her caring for him in the future? Did love mean he stayed, or did love mean he left?

"Linc?" Her light touch on his shoulder jolted him out of his thoughts.

Steeling himself for the sight of her, he turned.

"I'm going to hang out with Rosa while she packs. She wants to get out before the storm hits." She was already backing away. "With your team bunking in the dormitory tonight, I want to stay in her cabin so I can be available if they need anything."

Angie and Rosa had already planned to treat the NPS and FBI teams as though they were guests, providing food and lodging. Both agencies would pay a per diem, something Linc knew Angie desperately needed.

Well, if she was staying, so was he. She wasn't getting out of his sight, not when danger still lurked. They might suspect the serial killer was a cover for something else, but that still didn't explain who was after Angie. It wouldn't be the first time he'd bunked on a couch, and it wouldn't be the last.

But it might be the most uncomfortable. His neck still protested his snooze on Angie's sofa the night before.

He watched the door close behind her as the crime-scene units loaded the vans and shut the doors. They'd wait out the storm in the dormitory, then start again in the morning if the ground wasn't too saturated by the rain.

Thomas appeared at his side. He stood silently, watching

the weather before he finally spoke. "That was Detective Majenty from Coconino County. He put me on a conference call with the head of the FBI team."

Oh, no. Those players on one call meant either something very good or something very bad. Judging by the tone of Thomas's voice, it wasn't going to be good.

He faced Thomas as the wind pushed against his back, bringing the damp smell of rain.

Thomas pocketed his phone. "Coconino County and the FBI team are headed to Mac Dwyer's house."

His heart sank to his stomach. "They found Monica Huerta." He'd hoped it wouldn't end this way. That she had disappeared on her own and—

"No." Thomas scanned his phone screen. "Mac Dwyer's neighbor found him in the workshop behind his house."

Hope and grief lay heavy in Linc's stomach. How much more violence could they all take? "He's dead, isn't he?"

"Nearly. They're taking him to the hospital, but it doesn't look good." Thomas's expression was grim. "Linc, you may be right about there not being a real killer. This doesn't look like a suicide attempt or a straightforward murder. Somebody wanted information out of Mac. Just like Ellis, Mac Dwyer was tortured."

FOURTEEN

Rolling onto her side, Angie punched the pillow and stared at the thin curtains over Rosa's window. Without a clock and with her phone charging on the dresser, she had no idea what time it was. Given the way the darkness softened around the edges, she'd guess it was somewhere in the vicinity of five in the morning.

She held her breath, listening, but heard nothing. Something had snapped her out of a doze, but she couldn't place what it was.

There was no sound from Linc, who'd slept in the living room despite her offering to take the couch so he could have the bed. His back had to be killing him.

Maybe he had stirred and that's what she'd heard, but there were no further sounds. Given how lightly she'd been sleeping, it could have been anything from the breeze that blew between the buildings or a member of the FBI or NPS moving with the beginnings of the day.

What she wouldn't give for blackout curtains right about now. Rosa tended to live life the old-school way, starting her day with the sunrise and ending it with the sunset. She didn't let a clock dictate the rhythm of her life. She rolled along with nature.

That made zero sense. Angie flopped on her back. If she had her way, she'd ignore the outside world and sleep until her body decided it couldn't be still any longer. Given that she'd lain awake for the vast majority of the night and had only succumbed to a couple of catnaps, that could take several days.

No, sleep had not been her friend the previous night. Dark thoughts had chased it away, leaving her desperate for a mind that would simply be quiet for a few hours. Instead, she'd been plagued by images of serial killers, dead bodies and the all-too-real memory of a masked figure trying to drag her into the darkness.

How did investigators like Linc and her brother and Detective Blankenship deal with what they saw every day? This was the dark side of humanity, the worst of the worst.

Yet somehow, they managed to sleep at night.

She assumed. Maybe exhaustion claimed them when they dropped their heads on their pillows. Rest wasn't always sweet. She knew for a fact Jacob sometimes suffered from nightmares, and the way Linc talked, he did as well.

Her career as a meteorologist—sitting in front of her computer running calculations, or being in the field taking measurements—hadn't prepared her for this, nor had it allowed her to consider what others actually went through.

Why was Linc so upset about being unable to return to that life? Maybe helping catch the bad guys gave him a sense of peace.

What she wouldn't give for that right now.

Well, sleep wasn't going to come anytime soon, so she might as well start the day. While Thomas had left last night to process another scene with part of the NPS team, the FBI's crime-scene unit had remained on the property, planning to rise at first light to search for more hidden buckets.

Since they were paying to stay on the ranch, she should give them the full experience. Normally, Rosa set out a continental breakfast in the dormitory kitchen. With her gone, Angie could certainly start the coffee and set out the food.

As soon as the sun fully rose, she'd check in with Rosa to see how her mother was doing. Angie had spent part of the night praying for the family and their ongoing concerns.

Dressing quickly, she grabbed Rosa's keys off the nightstand and clipped them to her belt loop, then stepped to the door and eased it open, wary of disturbing Linc if he'd managed to fall asleep.

He was leaned back in the recliner by the cold fireplace, covered in a quilt.

Angie stepped closer, keeping her footfalls silent on the throw rug. If he was asleep, he needed to stay that way. Rest had been in short supply for the man who had given tirelessly of himself, ignoring his own needs to protect her.

The slack muscles in his face indicated he was deep in slumber. Without pain lines around his mouth and along his forehead, he looked like a younger Linc, one who didn't have the chains of a thousand violent crimes threaded through his mind.

Until now, seeing him completely oblivious to the world, she hadn't considered how much stress he carried. Piling his own pain and loss on top of it all had to weigh on him.

Yet he'd set himself aside to care for her.

The urge to plant a kiss on his forehead was almost overwhelming. She stepped back and shoved her hands into the pockets of her jeans, unable to look away.

At some point in the past few days, the awkwardness between them had melted. They'd become a team again. Friends.

Maybe something more.

The feeling that had been welling in her chest since he'd received that awful telephone call burst into bloom.

He'd kicked down the walls her behavior had built between them years ago. Now, together, they were building something different, something that looked like a solid foundation. Each brick they laid shored up the sense of rightness inside her.

The way he'd sacrificed himself to shield her.

The way he'd apologized for wounding her when he'd walked out in an effort to protect her years ago.

The way he'd been so careful with her emotions, stepping lightly in any situation that might remind her of her past struggles and wounded heart.

Her eyes slipped closed, and she reveled in the vision of Linc kneeling on the floor beside a child whose world had been flipped upside down, presenting her with a stuffed unicorn that lived in every little girl's dreams.

The man constantly thought of other people ahead of himself, and somehow, she was blessed enough to be one of the people in his orbit.

She balled her fists in her pockets and opened her eyes, staring at him as the thought bubbled from her heart. Linc was so much more than a friend.

He was now, as he had been when Jacob was injured, the man she'd fallen in love with.

It was too much to think about. Too much to dream for. Turning, Angie headed for the door.

What she needed was to get outside into fresh, rain-washed air and shake loose these thoughts. Linc cared about everyone. He set aside his needs for everyone. That was one of the reasons she'd fallen for him the first time.

She was nothing special.

Was she?

Surely he didn't hold on to everyone the way he'd held on to her. Didn't watch every woman as though she somehow both enchanted and confused him. No, there was something about the way he looked at her that said she might be more to him. That she hadn't wrecked the something special between them all those years ago.

Shaking her head, she turned the lock and eased the door open. Let Linc sleep. She couldn't deal with looking him in the eye right now anyway. If she did, breakfast would never appear for the team because she'd stop everything to wake him up and ask him point-blank how he felt.

Nothing could be more dangerous.

As silently as she could, she shut the door and stepped onto the porch, bumping into a planter Rosa had set beside the steps. It scraped across the floor loud enough to wake the dead.

She froze, cocking her head to listen, but no sound came from the house. *Good.* Linc needed to rest.

No lights were on in the dormitory, so the teams were probably still asleep. She could have coffee ready for them before they got moving. She knew from experience with her brother that law enforcement ran on caffeine and adrenaline. Hopefully, caffeine would be all they got today.

Unclipping the keys from her belt loop, she headed down the steps to make the short walk to the dormitory. The ground was still wet from the previous evening's storm, marked with boot prints from the barn around the corner of the cabin where Rosa's window was.

Angie slowed, her heart picking up speed. Linc had come inside at the same time as she had the night before, and the rain had just started to fall. Given the downpour had lasted a large chunk of the night, water would have washed away any footprints they'd left behind.

Someone had been outside this morning, but no one should have been around the cabin. They definitely shouldn't have been sneaking beneath her window.

She turned to race up the steps, but an arm snaked around her throat from behind, dragging her backward and putting pressure on her neck. She struggled, the keys clattering to the dirt, but her attacker held her fast.

Her pulse pounded in her ears.

Her breaths couldn't reach her lungs.

The sky grew dark.

Everything turned black.

* * *

Linc sat bolt upright, his neck screaming. A sound seemed to echo in his head, but he couldn't figure out what it was. A scrape? A roar? His imagination in overdrive?

Easing the recliner upright, he tried to stretch gently, regretting his decision to sleep in his pants and polo instead of going to the main house for his sweats. He felt grungy and warm, and he ached all over. The faster he got some food and ibuprofen into his system, the better.

He glanced at his watch. Nearly five. Angie would probably be champing at the bit to get to the dormitory to take care of coffee and breakfast. The night before, she'd promised to be over there before six. Surprising that she hadn't shaken him awake yet. He'd knock on the door and rouse her as soon as he woke enough to settle the unease in his subconscious.

He planted his feet on the floor and listened. Maybe that noise had been a dream, but something told him it wasn't. There was a *knowing* he'd developed through training and intuition that told him something wasn't right. He scanned the room as he shoved his feet into his boots, stood and reached for the gun he'd left beside him on the coffee table.

The bedroom door was open.

Outside, near the barn, a vehicle engine started and the sound quickly moved away from him.

Okay, *now* he was awake.

Linc raced to the bedroom door. The room was empty. He spun around and scanned the living area. "Angie?" There was no sign of her.

His heart picked up speed. She could be anywhere. Had probably gone to the dormitory to start breakfast. That vehicle driving away could have been one of the FBI agents heading out to get supplies.

His gut told him different.

He parted the curtains and peered out the window by the

door. Seeing nothing, he eased onto the porch, scanning the area in the milky predawn light. Nothing moved. The dormitory was dark and silent.

Flicking on his phone's flashlight, he searched the ground.

Footprints marred the recently dampened earth. One set was smaller—clearly Angie's, heading away from the cabin.

It was the second set that had him reaching for his phone. Men's boots. They circled the cabin and returned to the porch.

Since it had rained the night before, these were fresh, and no one on the government teams had a reason to be near the cabin.

Ignoring the larger set of prints, he followed Angie's toward the dormitory then stopped, rooted to the spot. The mud was scuffed and gouged, as though someone had struggled before being lifted from the ground.

He turned. The boot prints moving away from where he stood were deeper, as though the wearer bore a heavy load. The trail headed for the barn.

The barn. Where he'd heard an engine moments earlier.

He stopped, feeling like a deer frozen in headlights. Race after that vehicle? Or alert the teams?

As much as he wanted to give chase down the bumpy road, backup came first. Pressing the phone screen to dial Thomas, he raced for the dormitory and banged his fist on the locked outer door.

The windows lit as he roused the agents, who'd probably open the door armed and ready to roll.

Thomas answered the phone before any of the agents appeared, and Linc didn't wait for formalities. "Someone has Angie. I'm gathering the teams. They took off in a vehicle headed toward the main gate. No description."

The sound of motion crossed the line and Thomas muttered something under his breath that Linc probably didn't want to decipher. "On the way. Get the teams and get moving."

The door eased open and two of the agents, Sloane and

Mangum, pulled the door open wider and holstered their weapons when they realized it was Linc.

Before they could speak, he relayed the intel, then turned and ran for his truck, his heart pounding and his back protesting every step. Fear pulsed through him in a dangerous rhythm, adrenaline adding fuel to the frenzy.

Angie had to be okay. She had to be safe. She'd been right there, feet from him, and he'd lost her.

How?

He forced himself to breathe as he ran around the corner of the cabin, where he'd parked his truck. He couldn't let his emotions run the show, because that's how evidence was missed, mistakes were made and lives were lost.

Clicking the key fob, he glanced down and felt his world collapse.

The front driver's-side tire was flat. He ran up the path to the other vehicles and skidded to a halt, unable to comprehend what he was seeing.

Every vehicle had at least one useless tire.

There was no way to get to Angie.

FIFTEEN

Sheer panic rattled through Angie.

Consciousness returned in a rush, but her brain moved through a thick fog. Her body felt as though she was swimming in syrup.

She'd been dreaming about riding Chance through the trees, jostled by his gait. The colors were too bright. The sounds too loud. She'd jolted awake into darkness. The scent of grain overwhelmed her. The world had gone black. Her eyes were open, but there was nothing. Had she lost her vision? What was happening?

Her hands were wedged beneath her stomach, but she couldn't separate them. Her feet kicked, but they seemed to be bound. She tried to scream, but her body wouldn't cooperate. She was stuck inside something that covered her head, suffocating her. Stealing her thoughts. Controlling her emotions.

A low hum varied in intensity and pitch, sometimes louder, sometimes softer, and her body seemed to flow with it, out of her control.

Cold sweat coated her body, although she was horribly warm. She was trapped. No way out. No way to breathe. No way to scream. And dizzy. So dizzy.

Focus. She needed focus. If ever there was a time to force down her emotions, it was now, but panic raced through her mind and forced her body to fight her bonds. She had to get out. Had to get free.

Pain cut into her wrists but she couldn't gain movement. Nothing she tried worked.

The lack of oxygen and wild thrashing exhausted her rapidly and she dropped her head, suddenly numb. Her heart raced, but her body lacked the strength to fight and her brain lacked the energy to process.

Her head bounced against something, and clarity kicked in. This sound was familiar. The hum revved again. Was it a vehicle's engine? She rolled, trying to feel anything with her shoulders. The space was confined. She ran through images in her mind. A box. A trunk.

The floorboard of a pickup truck. One riddle solved. Somehow, the knowledge felt like a small amount of power.

Forcing herself to breathe slowly through her nose, she tried to remember how she'd gotten here. She'd been walking to the dormitory, following the footprints on the ground, when—

Panic surged her racing heartbeat. Whoever had been hunting her had finally captured her.

She'd been so foolish.

Her eyes slipped closed. It was so hot. So humid. If she could free her head from the heaviness that covered it, she could breathe. Her entire being craved fresh, cool air.

She never should have left the cabin without Linc. If she'd have shaken him awake, they'd be at the dormitory now. Safe.

Linc.

Unbidden tears slipped down her cheeks. If she got out of this, she'd have to tell him the truths she'd realized this morning. Her heart was incomplete without him.

She'd tell him... *If* she got out of this.

Her chance for survival was probably slim. It seemed likely no one had realized she was gone.

This was all her fault.

The vehicle slowed and negotiated a turn, then came to a stop. The hum died. The world rocked as a door slammed, pounding against her rising headache.

She should fight.

The door opened, and rough hands grabbed her ankles, dragging her across the bumpy floor. Fear turned her muscles into spaghetti, and her plans for freedom died.

There was no fight left. Only terror, regret and the foggy sense that reality was six seconds ahead of her.

Her captor threw her over his shoulder in a fireman's carry.

Adrenaline surged, driving her to struggle, but with a muttered curse and a grunt, the man pulled tight on her knees and drew her closer, hindering her movement. With fear robbing her strength and a lack of oxygen leaving her light-headed, Angie surrendered.

More than anything, she wanted to say *please*, but whatever covered her head reduced the word to a mumble. She hated to beg. Hated to show weakness.

The man hesitated, seeming burdened by her weight or by guilt. Maybe he was reconsidering. Hope flashed through her, giving volume to her utterances. *Please, don't do this.* The words were a series of whimpers, like the cries of a newborn calf.

His step stuttered, but then his shoulders straightened and he moved forward with renewed purpose.

Desperation drove Angie's thoughts, insisting she plead for her life, that she promise this man whatever he wanted, from selling the ranch to leaving the country, as long as he let her survive, but stubborn pride also rose, demanding she never give up.

She would not beg. She would not give her kidnapper the satisfaction.

She prayed as they seemed to be moving up a staircase. *Jesus, please. Please. Let Linc find me. Get me out of this.*

Her mind was fuzzy. Each step jarred against her diaphragm, making it harder to breathe in the already stifling, humid, recycled air.

Her breaths huffed faster. The air was too thick. Or she was panicking. Or dying. Or—

"Stop squirming before you throw me off balance and kill us both." The voice was a harsh hiss, barely above a whisper.

Either he was out of breath, or he was trying to disguise his voice. Still, something tickled a memory. She'd heard him speak before, but where?

She whimpered, trying to indicate how dangerously low her air supply was. Between the covering over her head and the pressure of his shoulder on her chest, her oxygen was so depleted that her throat barely squeaked.

The man's steps leveled, and he slid her from his shoulder. Her feet touched the ground for a moment before he shoved her to the hard floor, her back against a rough wall.

She tilted her head, trying to get air from beneath whatever covered her head. It felt like a bag and smelled heavily of grain and animal.

It had to be one of the horse's feed bags, from the ranch barn. Meant to keep oats fresh, the heavy bags were airtight and waterproof. She'd suffocate soon if it wasn't lifted. Although blessed cooler air floated from underneath, it wasn't enough. It would never be enough.

She tossed her head, trying to indicate her distress as she slumped over her bent knees.

Footsteps stomped closer, and the bag jerked away. Beautiful fresh air, clean and cool, washed over her sweat-dampened face. She gulped in deep lungfuls. Nothing had ever felt sweeter to her mind or body.

Her hair hung in her face and over her eyes, sticking to her lashes and irritating her skin. She tried to swipe it away, but her movements were clumsy. She stared at the floor between her knees.

Heavy boots were nearly toe to toe with her running shoes. Who was this man, and what did he want from her?

Slowly, dread climbing her spine, Angie lifted her head and faced her captor.

The delay could have cost Angie her life.

Linc's truck, the park-service SUV and the FBI van all had tires speared with what looked to be a wide blade. Likely Angie's abductor had been in a hurry and hadn't wanted to take the time to cut more than one tire on each, thankfully. It had taken ten minutes to change to spares, but the delay had surely allowed the other vehicle to reach the main road, and who knew which direction he'd gone after that?

He prayed Thomas and Detective Blankenship had been able to rally in time to get on the road. With no vehicle description, though, they'd have to rely on random checkpoints. Setting those up would take more time than they had, especially if the kidnapper was a local and took the less-traveled back roads.

The FBI team was sweeping the property, searching the barns and outbuildings, checking to see if the kidnapper had stayed close.

Linc prayed they had and Angie was found quickly. If not…

His brain didn't need to go there.

At the gate, he looked for protestors, hoping for witnesses, but no one was there. They hadn't returned after Riley's arrest.

While he'd disliked their presence before, he sure would love to see one of them now.

He rolled down his window to push the button on the keypad. As the gate swung open, he stared at the device.

Whoever had taken Angie had been driving a vehicle. The only way through the gate without Angie's remote was by punching in a code. He was fairly certain they'd exited through the main gate, but it was possible they'd entered that way as well.

Lord, let it be so.

If they'd entered through one of the padlocked back gates, then there was no way to know who it was. While no code was necessary to exit the main gate, maybe the camera had picked them up leaving. He'd heard the vehicle heading toward the main gate earlier, so perhaps they had a shot.

His heart surged and he uttered prayer after prayer. They might find Angie yet.

He roared through the gate with the federal teams behind him, punching the voice button on his steering wheel and practically shouting Rosa's name. Thankfully, he'd had the foresight to put her number into his phone the day before.

She answered on the third ring, sounding groggy. If she was caring for an ill parent, he might have interrupted her one shot at getting rest.

He winced, despite the urgency of the situation. "Rosa, I'm sorry to bother you, but I need help. Someone…" Should he tell her? In a rush, he exhaled. "Someone took Angie."

"What?" Her voice pitched higher, and the news had clearly startled her awake. "When? How?"

"No time to explain. I need to find out if anyone used a code to access the gate or if the camera caught footage of them leaving. Is that on your computer at the office?" If so, he'd have the FBI team access the data immediately. "Tell me how to—"

"I can check from my laptop to see everyone who's entered with a code. What time do you think they would have exited? That will help me isolate the video feed." As soon as he spoke an approximate time, the sound of fingers tapping on a keyboard clicked through the speakers, music to his ringing ears.

Linc gripped the steering wheel, kneading it with numb fingers. His back burned, and his shoulder throbbed. He was flying up the road toward the main highway, but he had no idea where he was headed.

All of his investigating had led him nowhere. No suspect. No motive. No idea who might have Angie or where they might have taken her. He could head to HQ, rally the troops, maybe—

"Linc?"

Hope rose at the sound of Rosa's voice. "Tell me you have something."

"No one has accessed the gate since you guys came in last night, although someone did leave less than half an hour ago. I can see that it opened, but there's no code required to exit."

"Is there a manual override to enter?" Maybe someone had managed to open it without the key code.

"No. It runs on solar, and if it does fail, it requires a key. Only Angie, Jacob and I have one. I'm checking the cameras now." More key taps, then a slight gasp. "The camera went down over two hours ago."

Pounding his fist against the steering wheel, Linc winced at the pain that rocketed up his arm. This had all been planned. Whoever had grabbed Angie this morning had set themselves up for success and then waited for their opportunity. "Someone came in the back way, but they knew this place well enough to disable the main cameras in order to take the fastest route back to the main road."

"I shouldn't have left."

The regret in Rosa's voice nearly undid him. "Don't beat yourself up. You need to take care of your mother." He'd been present in the cabin, and he'd failed to protect Angie. He'd been so focused on his pain and disappointment that he'd botched Angie's investigation and left her in danger.

Now he had nothing. "Thanks, Rosa. I'll keep you posted." Pressing the end-call button, he stared at the road ahead of him, navigating a curve at breakneck speed.

Now what?

A phone call shattered the silence, and his eyes went to the screen on his radio. *Rosa.* Praying she'd had an epiphany and hadn't accidentally redialed, he punched the button to answer. "Tell me you have something."

"I might." There was a muffled sound as Rosa spoke to someone away from the phone. "I'm getting my mom's phone to make a call. Stay on the line and trust me."

This was killing him. "What are you doing?"

"If you come in one of the back gates, you take the back roads, right? We don't have cameras on those gates, but at the end of the dirt road that leads to the south side of the ranch, there's a widow who lives alone in an older cabin, Selena Raymond. After someone broke into her car, probably tourists, her son installed one of those video doorbells. She complained to me it takes video of every car that drives by on the road, but she's never changed it because she's nosy enough to enjoy the show. Maybe—"

"Maybe Selena Raymond spotted our kidnapper."

"Hang on." There was a muffled conversation. Sparse words came through as Rosa spoke to Selena. "Text me. Quickly, please. Thank you."

She had something. "Talk to me, Rosa." He was nearing the main road and had choices to make.

"She's texting a screenshot to me. It should be here—" A gasp cut her words. "Linc."

"There's something usable, isn't there?" Adrenaline shot through him. There had better be. This was his only chance at finding the woman he loved before it was too late.

"A truck passed just before four this morning, and the floodlights on her house illuminated it perfectly. But, Linc? I recognize the truck."

SIXTEEN

Angie shrank against the wall. Surely she wasn't processing what she saw. This had to be wrong. The way her world was spinning, her mind had to be playing tricks on her.

But as he stepped back and her vision focused, she knew.

She tried to swallow, but her mouth was dry. If the shock wasn't so profound, she'd cry out her *why*.

Carter Holbert stared down at her, anger and angst in his expression. He jammed his hands into his dark hair and walked away. "This wasn't how it was supposed to happen." Gripping his head with his hands, Carter paced like a caged animal. "You couldn't just leave. You had to mess everything up."

Nausea gripped her, and Angie tried to breathe in and out through her nose. Adrenaline and panic crashed in her system, derailing her body. She forced herself to breathe slowly and deeply, to focus on anything other than the whirling inside and her inability to run.

Her eyes darted around the room. Recognition washed through her, temporarily dampening the nausea. The room was circular, with a low wall surrounding an open space in the center. Murals in the style of Hopi paintings covered the whitewashed walls. Heavy plastic sheeting hung over the windows. Scaffolding lined one wall and surrounded part of the central opening. The ceiling opened to the floor above, through which she could see the painted roof of the Desert View Watchtower.

Hope bloomed. If they were at the watchtower, tourists would be near the popular attraction. The historic area was—

Was closed.

Her stomach plummeted as though it had been thrown over the railing. Renovations to the Desert View Watchtower Historic District had the place fenced off so that visitors couldn't get near.

Like a horror-movie tagline, there was literally no one to hear her scream.

She leaned her forehead to her knees, her stomach roiling. Lifting her head, she tried to pull herself together before something horrible happened. Angie gulped air, silently begging God not to let her embarrass herself on top of everything else. She regulated her breathing until the nausea passed and cold sweat sheened her skin.

The battle left her weak.

She sagged against the wall and stared at Carter as he walked around the low center wall. "Why?" If she had the strength, she'd spout off more words, but she needed time to recover, to gather her wits and devise a plan.

She started working her wrists and hands, testing how secure the duct tape was. Given the numbness in her fingers, it was tight, which could work to her advantage. After he'd gone to SERE school, where the army taught how to escape and evade assailants, Jacob had taught her some tricks, including how to break duct tape and zip-tie bonds.

It took strength, an opportunity and prayer.

Lord, please let Linc figure this out. Let Carter make a mistake. Anything. Please.

A continual plea wound through her mind as she flexed her wrists and hands against the restraints. Why would Carter do this? What was—

Realization dawned, and her movements slowed. Carter had been digging on the property. He was connected to both

Isla and Monica. He'd been the first to mention a serial killer. "You murdered those women?" How? Carter had always been a friend of her family's. Yet all this time—

"What?" Carter whirled on her. Gone was the kind face she'd known. His forehead creased as his eyes narrowed. "I didn't kill those women. Ellis did. Him and his dad and Mac."

The words slapped against her ears, nearly toppling her. Shock shuddered through her. Ellis? Whom she'd hired to work on her ranch? His father, who'd been their first foreman and a cherished confidant of her father's? And Mac, the man who played Santa Claus?

"No." Her brain refused to assimilate the information. It was too far-fetched.

"They didn't actually kill anyone." Carter walked over and squatted before her, just out of reach. He studied her, seeming to weigh what he wanted to say.

Angie stared back, trying to read the truth behind familiar eyes. They were darker than she remembered, hard and cold.

Carter glanced away. "They made those women disappear."

Shaking her head, Angie bit her lower lip as the motion brought another wave of nausea. "They aren't kidnappers. You are."

"I am?" He spat the words, leaning closer, threatening her.

She wouldn't let him know he was terrifying. "I'm here, aren't I?" How could he not see what he'd done?

"And I'm willing to let you go free, if we cut a deal and you keep silent."

He had to know that would never happen.

"Ellis West's father, Javi, was some sort of bleeding-heart hero, I guess." Carter rocked back on his heels, settling in. "Those seven women who disappeared? Trouble, all of them. They were married to good men, or were working for good men. They didn't like to toe the line, so sometimes, they had to be set straight." He shrugged and stood, looking down at her with fire in his eyes.

"Set straight?" Angie's voice trembled, but she didn't falter, even though looking up at Carter made him more menacing. If he wanted, he could kill her with a swift kick.

It wasn't beyond the realm of possibility, not the way he was talking. She moved her wrists, forcing herself to slowly work the tape. If she moved too quickly, he'd notice and—

Angie swallowed a wave of fear. That was something she didn't want to consider, because the way he talked, those women had been abused, and Carter was supportive of that disgusting behavior from a man. He'd have no problem "setting her straight" if she caused "trouble."

"Those girls went to Javi and Mac. They faked those women's deaths. Made it look like they'd met somebody online who lured them away and killed them, then got them out of town, away from men who took care of them. At the time, nobody knew, but I finally figured it out." He smirked the satisfied smile of someone who'd outsmarted an enemy. "Isla and I had been together for a while when I saw on her cell phone that she'd been talking to somebody else. I asked her who, but she wouldn't tell me, no matter how much I tried to convince her."

Angie didn't want to know what his *convincing* might have looked like. "You were dating Isla? You beat her, didn't you?"

Carter's eyes blazed, and he stalked closer. He hulked over her, his booted feet a mere inch from her hip. "Isla is my business to handle." His fists balled and he stared down at her as though he was debating using them.

Angie looked away. Let him think she'd backed down, and maybe he'd keep talking. The longer he talked, the more time Linc had to find her.

He had to be worried about her.

Her heart wrenched. She should have told him she'd forgiven him and she… She loved him. If he didn't find her or she didn't escape, he'd never know.

Angie started flexing her wrists again. The duct tape slid a bit, and the friction burned her wrists, but she didn't dare stop. "What happened to Ellis?" There was no doubt Carter had killed Ellis, but why?

"When we were doing preliminary excavating about a month ago, I unearthed a bucket. It had some papers in it, and I thought the name was familiar, but I threw it in the truck and forgot about it 'cause we were busy working on this place." He glanced around the tower then turned to her. "Then Isla went missing, and the FBI started asking me questions, throwing names at me. One of them rang a bell, and it all came together. That serial killer a while back. The papers I found. They were from one of the missing women."

"But you didn't go to the police."

"I decided if I could figure out who'd buried that bucket, or maybe dig up some more of them, I could get some reward money out of the FBI. Couldn't hurt to wait a bit. Those women had been gone for years, so—"

"If you thought Isla was missing, that evidence could have saved her!"

Carter scowled. "It paid off, sort of." His expression darkened. "I looked around the property, but Rosa got suspicious, so I started to wonder… What if I could get you to sell me the ranch? I could search without questions, and once I got what I needed, I've got a developer on the hook who'd buy your place for a fortune. Wants to put up a resort. I'd profit pretty nicely."

Angie was going to be sick. Never had she imagined Carter could be so heinous.

"First I tipped off this little hippy nature organization and told them you wanted to build a resort. Thought they might scare you into selling, maybe be such a nuisance that you'd take off."

"I'm not leaving my family's land." He had to know that.

"It was worth a try. On the day you left for Vegas, Rosa was with her mother, I went to poke around a bit, and I saw Ellis with Monica Huerta. She'd been dating Syd O'Conner, and I thought she was maybe running around on him, but the next day, I saw she was on the news. It got me thinking."

"So you beat Ellis to death?"

He shot her a withering look. "Self-defense. With you gone for a week, I had time to figure out what I wanted to do. I gave it six days, then I called Ellis and told him to meet me at his cabin, that I was going to turn him in to the cops if he didn't talk to me. He had a postcard at the cabin that was in Isla's handwriting, and it was postmarked after she vanished. One I assume was from Monica, too. I guess that's how they let him know they'd gotten to wherever he'd sent them. I could have called the cops, but he'd helped Isla run away from me, and I wanted to know where she was. When it got…heated, I moved the chat over to your barn, since you were out of town and it was more private."

Angie clamped down on her tongue. Carter had killed Ellis while trying to find Isla.

"I can see you thinking." The haughty expression slipped, and fear skittered across Carter's face. "I never meant for Ellis to die, but he wouldn't give me the answers I wanted. By the time he did, the damage was done. He told me about his dad and Mac before he passed out."

"You mean before he died."

Carter shrugged. "I heard your car come back, and I thought…maybe I can scare her into selling. Turns out you don't scare easy." Carter stared at his hands, then shook his head as if to clear it. "Ellis told me that Mac and Javi had hidden the other girls' identification documents around the ranch in case they ever wanted to return to their lives. Mac had a map, but he wouldn't give it to me." Carter walked away and stood at a window as though he could see through the opaque plastic. Likely he was trying to erase the vision of what he'd done to Ellis and to his friend Mac.

While his back was turned, Angie twisted her hands, loosening the duct tape as her wrists burned and chafed. It was loose enough that maybe, if Carter remained distracted, she could slam her hands over her knee and rip the tape.

When Carter turned, she froze.

"I want to buy the ranch and find the rest of those documents. Might be some clues in there to lead those men to the women who did them wrong. If nothing else, it'd let them have proof they were done dirty. I bet they'll pay quite a bit to know their women are still alive." He looked down at her. "You have two choices." He squatted and grabbed her chin. "You can disappear and your ID can show up bloodied on your mama's doorstep. You start a new life, and I buy the ranch since your brother would never tackle trying to run it without you." He squeezed tighter, pinching her skin. "Or…"

There was no need to finish the sentence. Either she walked away from everything she knew…

Or Carter committed one final murder.

"Send someone to Carter Holbert's home and someone else to his business." As sunrise painted the sky in pink and orange streaks, Linc raced toward Tuba City nearly an hour away, where Carter lived and had an office. "Hopefully he's taken her there."

"It's a long shot, Tucker. There's a lot of places he could be." Thomas was a realist, never one to offer false hope.

"It's all I've got. Coconino County is out searching, and the FBI team is scouring the ranch, but…"

"We'll find her. I know what she means to you. Always have. We won't let you down." Thomas ended the call before Linc could respond.

"Nobody knows what she means to me." He sped on, scanning side roads for evidence of recent activity. Carter Holbert could have driven any number of places on the rim of the canyon, could be deep in the forest...

And he had the woman Linc loved.

How had Thomas known when he hadn't even figured it out for himself until a few hours earlier? Likely because Linc had always loved her, and working with investigators who were both observant and intuitive made secrets tough to keep.

If he'd been intuitive about his own emotions sooner, maybe none of this would be happening now.

He pushed up the two-lane road toward the park exit, determined to reach Tuba City, and—

Wait.

His focus froze on a brown park-service sign illuminated in his headlights. He'd nearly passed it before the words registered, and he slammed on the brakes, the rear of the truck fishtailing before it stopped.

Desert View.

Linc stared at the sign. Desert View Watchtower was the next left.

Carter Holbert was a contractor working on the renovations to the tower. The historic area around the landmark was closed during the restoration. No tourists. No traffic.

But Carter had access.

It was the perfect place to hide.

Gunning the engine, Linc took the left turn and barreled up the road past the parking lot that led to the visitors' center, seeking the construction entrance.

There. What amounted to a small dirt road was flanked by signs that labeled the area a construction zone. The barriers that blocked the entrance had been moved aside, the drag marks evident in the mud.

Killing the engine, Lincoln studied the rough ground.

Someone had pulled a vehicle onto the makeshift drive since the rain the previous night. This had to be the place.

He should notify Thomas.

No, he needed proof before he pulled anyone away from their assigned search area. If he was wrong, the detour would be a waste of valuable time.

As the sky brightened, Linc turned off the sound on his phone, shoved it into his pocket, checked his SIG and left his vehicle quietly. He crept toward the tower, keeping to the shadows. If Carter had Angie inside, he had the height advantage and a view of the entire surrounding area.

Linc slowed as the tower came into view. An impressive structure, it rose from the landscape at the edge of the canyon, as though it had been there since the dawn of time, created naturally from the rocks.

The canyon opened before him in a spectacular vista of light and shadow as the sun peeked over the horizon. The sky rioted with pink, orange and purple as night faded to day.

At any other time, the view would steal his breath.

But another sight entirely caught him in the chest. Carter's pickup was parked near the tower's entrance.

Linc ducked into the shadow of a small tree and texted Thomas. Found Carter's truck. Desert View Watchtower. Going dark. Shoving his phone into his pocket, he studied the tower, searching for the best avenue of attack.

Built to look like an oversize Puebloan watchtower rising from rubble at the rim, the century-old structure afforded visitors spectacular views. It also gave Carter a vantage point to watch for their approach.

Construction equipment and supplies dotted the area, and the tower's windows appeared to be sealed off by plastic sheeting for protection during the renovation.

Thanks to that, he might be able to gain access without being seen, though he had no idea where Carter was holding Angie in the building. If they were on one of the upper levels, the open center of the tower would provide Carter a direct view down to the first floor. If Linc could get to the stairs, it would be possible to make his way up hidden by the half wall that lined the stairs as they twisted around the exterior walls of the building.

If only he could be invisible.

Linc crept to the truck and cleared the vehicle before moving cautiously toward the tower's heavy wooden door. A padlock was lying on the ground, useless to anyone on the inside.

SIG at the ready, Linc eased the door open inch by inch, braced for attack.

When no assault came, he slipped inside and pressed his back to the wall. The ground floor was empty, the gift shop sheeted in plastic to protect against the dust of construction.

"What's your decision?" A deep voice rumbled from above, close to the southwest wall.

Muscles pulsing with stress and pain, Linc eased toward the stairs. He crouched behind the low wall on the interior of the stairs, trying to gauge if Carter was the lone assailant and praying the question had been addressed to Angie.

Hunched low, Linc crept up, one slow, nightmarish step at a time.

"I won't let my family think I'm dead." Angie's voice, strong and defiant, wafted down from the opening in the floor.

Linc's muscles relaxed so quickly, they nearly puddled him to the stairs. She was alive.

For the moment.

"They can *think* you're dead, or you can actually *be* dead." Impatience laced Carter's words, as though Angie had been stalling for time.

Good job. She had to have known he'd come for her, that somehow he'd find her.

He had to move quickly if he was going to save her. Carter sounded as though he was done waiting.

Near the top of the stairs, Linc stopped, wary of exposing his position. He stretched his body out over the last three steps, his head nearly on the floor, and peered around the base of the wall that separated the stairs from the circular second floor.

In the center of the room, scaffolding stood on one side of the low retaining wall around the open center of the building. At the one-o'clock position, Angie sat on the floor, her face white with fear.

Linc drew back. Where was Carter?

He scanned the visible area, seeing nothing. He should wait for backup, but time wasn't on his side. If Angie died while he was within feet of her—

Linc forced himself to focus. That kind of thinking would only paralyze him. He shook it away, then eased to the top of the stairs and crouched, ready to round the corner and spring, although he was blind to Carter's whereabouts.

Weapon drawn, he rose, prepared to shout Carter's name.

The plastic sheeting rustled, and Carter leaped from the blind spot behind the scaffolding, driving Linc backward to the floor.

SEVENTEEN

"Linc!"

Angie gasped as Carter slammed Linc to the floor. Linc's gun clattered to the ground and skittered beneath the scaffolding several feet away.

Carter raised a fist to pound Linc's head, but Linc rolled onto his shoulder.

Carter's knuckles slammed the ground. He roared in pain as Linc shoved him away and scrambled unsteadily to his feet, his face pale and his expression tight.

The fall had likely caused him further injury. How much more could his spine take? A fight like this was the very thing his doctor had warned him about.

She had to do something.

As Carter rose to one knee, Linc swung and caught him in the chin.

Carter dove for Linc's knees, forcing him onto his lower back.

She couldn't stand by any longer. Carter could paralyze Linc before her eyes.

Lifting her hands, Angie pulled her palms as far apart as the loosened duct tape would allow and slammed them over her bent knee.

Her first blow landed to one side, the impact firing pain into her left wrist.

Carter landed another punch and scrambled across the floor

toward Linc's pistol as Linc appeared to shake off more pain. He grabbed Carter's ankle and pulled, bracing against the wall. "Angie! Get out!"

There was no way she was leaving him. She ignored the pain in her injured wrist and brought her hands down again. This time, her knee drove between her palms and ripped the duct tape. She twisted and pulled, her wrists burning, until the weakened bonds tore free. She moved quickly to unwrap her ankles.

Her left hand screamed with pain and the skin was already turning blue. Could she save Linc if she'd fractured her wrist trying to free herself?

Carter rolled and kicked upward, but Linc dodged and avoided a boot heel to the face. He threw himself over Carter's legs and tried to stop the man from getting closer to the gun.

The last of the duct tape pulled free, and Angie leaped to her feet. She raced around the low central wall, away from the men, hoping to come around on the other side of the circular room to grab the pistol before Carter could reach it.

Carter struggled to his feet.

Linc rose with him, but he moved much slower.

It was the advantage Carter needed. He shoved Linc toward the thigh-high central wall.

Linc stumbled. The top of his body pitched over the wall.

"Carter!" Angie screamed the man's name, hoping to distract him. She reached the gun and scooped it from the ground, straightening as she raised the weapon.

It was too late.

As he fell, Linc flung his arm out and wrapped his elbow around the scaffolding. He hung on, dangling two stories above the ground.

A fall wouldn't kill him, but given his injuries, it could paralyze him.

Carter lunged forward to pry Linc from the scaffolding.

Angie steadied the pistol. "Back away, Carter, or I'll pull the trigger."

This time, Carter seemed to hear her. He froze, arms extended toward Linc as though suspended between a decision about finishing off his opponent or taking a bullet if he tried.

Linc's face was white with pain as he attempted to throw his leg over the wall.

The scaffolding shifted, off balance due to his added weight, and threatened to topple over the edge with him. He froze, and his gaze pierced Angie's. "Get out."

She shook her head. If she knew Linc, he hadn't rushed in here alone. He'd called for backup, and help was on the way. All she had to do was keep Carter at bay until they arrived.

Carter held his hands away from his sides, his expression neutral. "Angie, I know you. You wouldn't shoot me."

She ground her teeth together. "And I *thought* I knew you." Carter had already killed once and attempted to kill a second time. He had nothing to lose. She wasn't about to let him add Linc to the list.

"Angie, don't." Linc's voice was strained. He reached for the wall, but the scaffolding creaked and swayed.

Carter eased closer to Linc. "Put the gun down." His arm rose slightly, moving toward the metal frame. "Put it down or I shove the scaffolding and your boyfriend over the edge."

Angie refused to move. If she put the gun down, Carter would kill them both.

Quick as a striking snake, Carter lunged.

Angie fired.

Carter jerked. He stopped, stumbled toward her, then dropped to his knees, staring down at his right side. Blood seeped through his shirt in a quickly spreading stain. He lifted his gaze to hers, eyes wide with panic and disbelief.

She couldn't believe she'd pulled the trigger, either, but there wasn't time to consider her actions.

Shoving the pistol into her waistband, she ran the long way around to avoid Carter and grabbed the scaffolding, keeping one eye on Linc and one on Carter. "I'll hold the scaffolding. You get over the edge." She leaned back with all of her weight, counterbalancing his.

To her left, Carter stirred. If he charged, there would be nothing she could do. Letting go would plunge Linc to his death. Ignoring Carter could allow him to shove them both over the edge.

She held on tight.

Linc managed to pull himself closer to the circular balcony, then he threw his chest over the low wall.

Releasing the scaffolding, Angie helped him the rest of the way. When he was on solid ground, she turned to Carter.

He'd stood, one hand braced on the wall and the other pressed to his side over the wound. "You should have killed me."

He sprang before she could reach for the pistol.

"Stop! Federal agents!" Multiple voices rang out from the stairs.

Angie whirled.

Carter stumbled, then froze.

Thomas approached, followed up the stairs by several other agents.

Every ounce of breath left her.

It was over.

Angie dropped to her knees beside Lincoln, resting her forehead against his shoulder as men and women swarmed into the room.

Linc dropped his head against the wall, but he didn't reach for her.

Somehow, she'd assumed he'd pull her close or check to see if she was okay.

Instead, he was still and silent.

She backed away and took his cheeks in her hands. She'd

Hidden in the Canyon

promised herself if she saw him again, she'd tell him the truth about her feelings. It didn't matter the place was swarming with law enforcement. It didn't matter they were seconds removed from certain death.

All that mattered was they'd survived, and she wouldn't go another moment without saying what was in her heart before the chance was ripped away again. "Linc, I—"

"No." He looked past her. Grasping her wrists, he pulled her hands from his face. "Angie, please." His jaw was set. His eyes were cold. "Don't."

"I know we've been—"

"Don't." The word was jagged. As though his body was encased in concrete, Linc braced himself against the wall and stood. He met Thomas a few feet away, said something to him, then made his way to the stairs and slowly disappeared down them as Thomas approached her, his expression grim.

They'd been saved. She was safe. Lincoln should be relieved.

They should be celebrating one another.

Instead, he was walking away.

He was sick and tired of his stupid apartment in employee housing. His stupid physical therapy. His stupid everything.

Linc tossed a frozen meat-loaf dinner into the microwave and slammed the door. Since he'd started daily PT two weeks earlier, the exercises and the pain ate his energy and his will to do anything more than exist.

At least he seemed to be physically improving. They might even let him return to limited duty behind a desk eventually. The blow he'd taken in the watchtower, when Carter had knocked him onto his back, had done additional damage to his spine.

It had been the very thing his doc had warned him about.

It wasn't like he went toe-to-toe with bad guys every day, or even every year, but if it happened again—

The microwave beeped as someone knocked on his door.

Linc froze in the kitchenette. If he was super still, maybe they'd go away.

It could be Angie. She'd called him until he'd blocked her number. Had come to see him the first couple of days after his overnight stay in the hospital.

He hadn't acknowledged her knock then, but maybe she'd worked up the courage to try again.

Jacob had reached out when he returned from Europe, but Linc had ignored her brother as well. He wasn't ready to answer questions.

His visitor knocked louder. "Tucker, I know you're home. I heard the microwave. Open up, or I'll claim probable cause and bust in."

Thomas.

Linc made his way to the door, his back and neck throbbing a reminder that the damage might be permanent.

Pulling the door open, he blocked the entrance and glared at his teammate. "Make it quick, I'm about to eat."

Thomas smirked. "Aren't you just a brilliant burst of sunshine."

"What do you want?" If Thomas was looking for hospitality, he wasn't going to find it here. "You want happy people, go hang out with tourists."

"I brought you a wake-up call." Thomas stepped aside and someone moved in front of him.

Linc wanted to slam the door.

Jacob Garcia squeezed past him into the apartment, invading Lincoln's space. "I figured you weren't talking to anyone with the last name Garcia, so I had Thomas run interference." The words were hard, and his closest friend's face was a thundercloud.

Tough to determine if it was because Linc had been ignoring Jacob, or because he was ignoring Jacob's sister.

Thomas stepped in, shut the door behind him and made himself comfortable on the couch while Jacob stood in the center of the living room, arms folded over his chest. He looked ready for a fight.

Lincoln would give him one. He matched Jacob's posture, though crossing his arms caused him pain. "Whatever happens between me and your sister is between me and her." Although not talking to her was costing him everything. He thought about her all day and through the dark nights.

There was no denying he loved her, but love changed nothing. It was better for her future if he stayed away. Saddling her with a ticking time bomb of medical issues like himself wouldn't be fair. She deserved a whole man.

As Thomas watched from the couch like a spectator at a boxing match, Jacob tilted his head. "This is about you, *battle buddy*." He hit those last two words with heavy sarcasm. Jacob and Linc had trained together and been to war together, carrying one another through situations most people wouldn't see in their nightmares.

The term took the starch out of Linc's fight. He looked toward the microwave, where his meat loaf was likely congealing into a gelatinous blob.

Maybe Jacob had a point. Linc had been stewing in his pain, refusing to reach out for help. Bad things happened when a man got into his own head, when pride kept him isolated.

He'd lobbed that exact lecture like a grenade one night when Jacob had turned his face to the wall and declared his life was over, that he was a broken man who'd never fully live, who couldn't have a child and might as well put his dreams out to pasture.

Jacob exhaled loudly. "You're hearing your own words in your head right now, aren't you?"

"It's annoying when you think you can read my mind."

"We've been through enough together that I've earned the right."

Linc stared down the friend who was closer than a brother. For the first time in weeks, something besides self-pity and anger wound through him. Maybe it was friendship. Maybe it was hope.

Jacob leaned against the back of the couch. "I remember being in so much pain I couldn't remember my own name. Some nights I thought death would be preferable to the pain. I knew I was done with the army. I thought I'd never function again."

Linc couldn't look at him or at Thomas, who watched silently. "I remember." There had been moments he'd been afraid his friend would never recover. That no matter how much he and Angie tried to pour hope into Jacob, he'd wither away.

Today Jacob was nearly as strong as he'd been before the explosion. He worked on Linc's investigative team and, in a twist no one saw coming, was married with a child of his own.

"All of those things I'd assumed I'd lost, God restored." Jacob sniffed. "Not to be harsh, man, but you're not nearly as bad off as I was."

Lincoln winced. This was true.

"Dude, it's time to stop feeling sorry for yourself." Jacob leaned forward slightly. "And, yeah, it's time to stop torturing my sister."

He'd known this was coming. "You have no idea."

From the couch, Thomas finally spoke. "Clue us in."

Anger rose, but Linc swallowed it. The last thing he needed was an argument when he wanted understanding. "In the heat of battle, I couldn't save Angie. *She* had to rescue *me*."

"So your male ego is bruised?" Dropping his hands to his sides, Jacob straightened. "You're going to hurt Angie because your *pride* is wounded?"

"No." The word fired out like a bullet. "You don't under-stand. I could be an invalid someday. A car wreck or a fight with a suspect could paralyze me. No offense, Jacob, but I took care of you right beside Angie. It was tough, physically and emotionally. I won't put her through that."

"So unless you're perfect, you won't marry her?"

Linc's head jerked. Pain fired down his spine. "Who men-tioned marriage?" Certainly not Angie. She didn't jump the gun that way.

"I did." Thomas stood. "You're in love with her. She's in love with you. You two handle each other quite well."

"None of us are idiots." Jacob had the audacity to chuckle. "You've been in love with my sister for years."

"I—"

"Don't even start." Jacob shook his head, a half smile on his face. "Remember how you stood in my barn and told me the whole platoon knew I was in love with Ivy? They all felt like she was their little sister and took her side when I didn't fight for her?"

Yeah, he could vividly remember thinking Jacob was an idiot for not confessing his love to the woman he was clearly meant to be with. "How much of my advice are you going to throw in my face today?"

"All of it." Jacob arched an eyebrow and lowered his voice. "Because this time I really am the brother, and I really do take her side."

Emotion shoved at the back of Linc's throat. He loved Angie and had for nearly as long as he'd known her. "I don't want to hurt her." Great. He'd resorted to whining.

"Life can be painful, Tucker." Thomas fully joined the con-versation. "Marriage isn't easy. You stand in front of God and everybody, and promise to love each other no matter what. 'In sickness and in health' isn't something to be taken lightly, I get it, but any of us could go down anytime to anything.

Car wreck. Heart attack. Gunshot. Life is risky. You take the risk and love someone you might lose. You take the risk they could lose you. *Or* you live alone and bitter in a government apartment, eating smelly frozen dinners and binge-watching car shows."

"You're a pain in the rear when you get like that." Jacob wasn't pulling punches. "You're not special. Love is a risk for everyone, not just for you and Angie. Maybe you'll work a desk job for the rest of your life. Maybe you'll get back into the canyon someday. Maybe a meteor will hit you in the head five minutes from now. Nobody knows, but you trust God and go for it. You promise to love no matter what. You make that promise *because* you don't know what's going to happen. If we knew what was going to happen, we wouldn't have to trust God."

That one hurt. Linc liked to think he was a guy who put his faith in God, but he sure wasn't acting like it.

He looked from his microwave to his teammates.

From his past to his future.

Maybe it was time to start.

EIGHTEEN

The sky was streaked with feathery cirrus clouds that glowed like living fire as the sun sank toward the horizon. Sunset on the ranch felt sacred. The light was different here, where the land ran dotted with trees to the canyon's rim.

If only the peace here could heal her broken places.

Angie had opened up, let go of control and allowed herself to feel, and all she'd earned was pain.

Stepping down into the foundation of what would someday be a dormitory, she sat on the edge and braced her feet against the hard earth, staring at the hole where they'd found the original bucket. When Mac had awakened in the hospital, the FBI had been waiting with questions. While Angie hadn't been privileged to all of the information from that interview, he had clearly given them a list of coordinates for every bucket on the ranch. The agents had collected them without telling her anything, but she was smart enough to figure out that their actions confirmed what Carter had suspected. The women who were supposedly murdered by a serial killer had actually vanished of their own accord. Given that they'd left voluntarily, locating them would probably not be a priority.

It was likely that none of them wanted to be found anyway.

When news broke of Carter's arrest, Isla Blake came out of hiding in Texas. The rest of the women would probably stay where they were. Their abusers were still a threat.

It was heartbreaking to think a person could be so frightened of a loved one that they were willing to disappear, yet it had happened over and over.

With Carter in jail, Angie would have to restart the bidding process, which delayed the new research center. It might give her time to line up financing, though that had taken a turn as well.

Owen had called a few days earlier. Her ex had apologized and had offered to align his foundation with her research center, opening a world of new funding.

While the apology settled more easily than Angie had thought it would, the situation would take prayer. While she'd managed to forgive him, forgetting would be difficult. She'd asked him to give her time. Maybe she could work with him, maybe not. The answer was up to God.

So was her relationship with Lincoln.

The raw space in her heart had his name etched into it. Since he'd walked away in the tower, it was as though he'd vanished. Her calls went straight to voice mail. Her knocks on his door went unanswered.

They were both safe, yet he'd ghosted her. No updates. No explanations.

Yep, she'd opened her heart and it hurt worse than any pain Owen had ever inflicted.

Angie frowned. It wasn't fair, yet she was determined not to close herself off. God had built her to be a whole person, not one who denied her feelings and sabotaged her joy. As much as it hurt, she was going to let the feelings run their course.

"Is this a private sunset viewing or can anybody join?"

Angie jerked around and jumped to her feet, nearly stumbling backward into the excavated foundation.

Linc stood not six feet away, his hands in his pockets, his brown hair tousled by the breeze.

Her heart pumped sparks to her fingers and burned through

her voice. Part of her had honestly started to believe she'd never see him again.

Now here he was.

All she could do was stare as emotion pulsed behind her eyes. Was she really going to cry?

Turning away from him, she faced the west, where the day was about to melt into night.

The next thing she knew, he was at her side, close enough to feel his warmth. He said nothing, merely watched the sun kiss the horizon as the sky roared with vibrant color.

After two weeks of silence, his presence was overwhelming. "Why are you here?" She looked at him from the corner of her eye, scared to fully face him for fear of igniting something in her heart she no longer wanted to feel if he was going to abandon her.

Linc inhaled slowly, as though his words needed oxygen to bring them to life. He watched her instead of the sky. "Honestly?"

"That would be nice."

He laid a hand on her shoulder and turned her toward him, pinning her gaze with his blue eyes. "I don't want to make the same mistake twice."

She was going to cry. There was no way around it. Her throat ached and her eyes burned. The breeze blew a wisp of hair across her face, but she couldn't swipe it away. She was scared to move, scared he'd spook like a wild horse. She was on the edge of having what her heart had always dreamed of, and she was terrified her instincts were wrong.

Linc's expression softened as his gaze roamed her face. "I walked away once because I was afraid I'd hurt you if I stayed, and I recently realized I'm doing the same thing again." He swept his index finger across her cheek, tucking the errant wisp of hair behind her ear. His eyes followed the motion as his fingers trailed lightly from her ear to the dip between her shoulder and her neck, making her skin tingle. "I was wrong both times."

Her eyes closed and she bit her bottom lip to keep the tears in check.

"Hey." He slipped his fingers to her chin and tilted her head. "I want you looking at me when I say the next part."

Opening her eyes allowed the tears to gather, but they didn't fall. She watched, waiting for him to speak, praying the words would be what she wanted to hear.

He looked down at her with a kind of wonder. "I think we've proven we can get through anything together." His voice was husky. "I want to go through it all together, from here, right on until we both breathe our last. Looking out for each other. Loving each other." He tilted his head, and the conviction in his expression nearly undid her. "I do love you, and I don't know what's going to happen next, but I truly, more than anything I've ever wanted in my life, want to do forever with you."

He was killing her, but he was doing it in the best of ways. Her heart was going to wreck itself any second.

If she went out right now, at least she'd be with him. She swallowed, trying to will her voice into existence. "I really, truly, more than anything in my life, want to do forever with you, too."

He smiled in a way she hadn't seen in years. When she slipped her arms around his waist, he drew her closer, running his fingers into her hair, meeting her halfway in the kiss they should have shared the first time. One that gave instead of took. One that promised love and honor and more… Walking through the good and the bad together… Forever.

* * * * *

Dear Reader,

When Angie and Linc appeared in *Witness in Peril*, she acted awfully strange about him. I knew they had a history, so I thought it might be fun to explore. I hope you enjoyed walking through their story with me!

Angie particularly intrigued me, because her struggle is one I was dealing with. I have a habit of charging through hard times without stopping to feel them. I keep my eye on the task, never letting emotions catch me.

That's not healthy. As Ecclesiastes 3 tells us, there is a time for everything in life, good and bad. We live in a spectrum of experiences, from gloriously wonderful to horribly difficult. When we refuse to feel the "hard" things, we dampen our ability to feel the good. God wants us to experience the fullness of His joy, something we can only do when we trust Him in all times. Trusting Him means believing the outcome is in His hands, believing He walks beside us.

Our family has walked a difficult road lately, and God is teaching me how to deal with it in healthy ways. That allows me to feel the happy times more…like this past week when my daughter and new son-in-law said "I do!" I pray we learn to trust God in beauty and in ashes. That's the full range of life. We're blessed to have a God who walks with us!

I'd love to hear from you and about any of the recent joys in your life! Drop by jodiebailey.com to share!

Jodie